Praise for Joely Skye's
Lynx

"With an intensity that will you breathless, Lynx hits the mark in every way."

~ *Kimberley Spinney*

"The suspense, sensual encounters and emotional rollercoaster rides are what will do you in with this story."

~ *Literary Nymphs*

"I not only recommend this story but plan to read it again soon."

~ *Rainbow Reviews*

"Lynx is a fantastic, and dark, paranormal romance. Jonah's evolution...makes for a fascinating read."

~ *Joyfully Reviewed*

"I could not put it down until the very last page. Ms. Skye makes you feel like you are there with Trey and Jonah..."

~ *Whipped Cream Reviews*

"The characters were well drawn and the intensity of the interaction between the heroes was absorbing."

~ *Jessewave*

"Ms. Skye has written a fast paced story with paranormal characters that come to life for the reader."

~ *Fallen Angel Reviews*

Look for these titles by
Joely Skye

Now Available:

The Minders Series
Monster
Zombie
Minder

The Minder Series in Print
Beautiful Monster

Marked
Poison
Feral
Wolf Town

Lynx

Joely Skye

Samhain Publishing, Ltd.
577 Mulberry Street, Suite 1520
Macon, GA 31201
www.samhainpublishing.com

Lynx
Copyright © 2011 by Joely Skye
Print ISBN: 978-1-60928-015-4
Digital ISBN: 978-1-60504-975-5

Editing by Sasha Knight
Cover by Mandy M. Roth

First Samhain Publishing, Ltd. electronic publication: April 2010
First Samhain Publishing, Ltd. print publication: February 2011

Dedication

To my editor, Sasha, who *always* makes my books better.

Chapter One

Trey was three days deep into the Canadian Shield—it was slow progress going uphill towards a major ridge in a snowstorm—when he recognized he was being tracked. The whiff of a predator too faint to identify. The muffled echo of something moving over the snow's surface.

He'd come here on a whim, investigating the odd report of a giant lynx in the area—though giant lynxes were long extinct. Didn't matter, this was his idea of vacation. He hadn't expected to discover much of anything. He certainly hadn't expected to be tracked by another animal, and this new development invigorated him.

The bone-deep weariness that had afflicted Trey these past weeks vanished. Easy as that it was gone. Instead he faced a challenge, one only his wolf had to deal with—identify his tracker. It had nothing to do with humans and their world, nothing to do with his work. Just the wilderness and his wolf and this snowstorm.

Trey decreased his speed, as if he were ailing in some fashion, as if he were weak. With a potential predator on his trail, such a strategy might flush him out. Predators were a curious bunch, by and large, and they liked to take advantage of weakness.

Usually, amended Trey hours later, when no predator had

yet appeared. After half a day of this, Trey became impatient with his slow progress, given that his tracker continued to keep its distance. Perhaps it wasn't hungry, never mind that they were in the dead of winter. True, Trey wasn't hungry, but he'd feasted a number of times over the past few days and had been well nourished before he'd set out. This animal was unlikely to have the same advantage.

Possibly it wasn't a predator, but Trey was hard-pressed to imagine a deer or hare following him. Besides lacking basic brainpower, they were timid, fearful creatures that didn't like to bring a wolf's attention to themselves.

What if it's not just an animal? Unbidden, the thought grabbed hold, as did the idea of a shifter. Interest piqued, Trey decided to take a more proactive approach. Picking up speed, he veered left and began doubling back, going wide. It took some time but eventually he crossed tracks, not too old.

The fur on the back of his neck rose in anticipation. He observed incredibly large prints with no claw marks—classic lynx tracks except they were too big, even for their snowshoe paws. Cat shifters were rare and usually cougar in form. So what were the chances of a *lynx* shifter? Let alone a giant lynx.

Trey was fascinated and excited, as if he were about to discover a whole new continent. Still, it was important to think this through. Animal or werecat, the creature might be dangerous, vicious. A terrible shame if it was the latter, but a possibility he had to be prepared for as he followed its trail.

His tracking was slower than he liked. The snow was too soft, too deep, for his paws. He could have stayed human and used snowshoes so he didn't continually sink into the powdery snow. But human form meant more thinking than he chose to deal with on vacation.

The wind increased, and more than once he almost lost the trail as it got covered at times by blowing snow. The lynx was moving quickly now; its huge paws kept it mostly above the drifts. After a while, the hunt became exhausting and if Trey wasn't careful he'd get in trouble, so he paced himself and kept alert.

Farther on it became evident that the lynx had become aware of him. Its route turned convoluted as it backtracked a couple of times and used some tree-climbing as a diversion.

But this show of intelligence wasn't the only thing that had Trey's anticipation growing. As the area became sheltered by the huge rock face, he finally gained on the lynx and picked up its scent in the prints it left behind. And though he'd never before identified a lynx shifter, this one did not scan as pure animal.

Trey stopped and threw back his head to howl. Whether the shifter would recognize it as a greeting, he didn't know, but there was no harm in trying to say hello before they actually met up.

The sun's dim light faded and dusk was almost upon him before Trey reached the cover of the rock face and the snow no longer blew past him. He was close now, so he paused to gather the rest of his energy. His excitement at finding a new kind of shifter had to be balanced with some caution. Even if lynxes were known as shy creatures who hid more than they attacked.

The wolf had, of all things, turned the tables and was stalking him. Early in the day, Jonah had come upon it and enjoyed watching it, as he did much of the wildlife around him. To his mind, wolves were particularly beautiful creatures.

He hadn't wanted to get too close and rattle it—lone wolves had enough worries. But then its progress had slowed significantly in the late morning, and he'd wondered if it was injured. While he'd been worrying about its state of health and keeping an eye on it, the wolf had suddenly disappeared. So

11

he'd shrugged off its injury and his losing its trail, and figured the wolf was fine after all. As Jonah headed home he slowly realized *it* was tracking *him*. Now this wolf was almost at his front door.

The about-face made Jonah feel strange. This switch was outside his experience. Wolves were smart, sure, but this was quite extraordinary. And truth was, apart from Eliza, wolves steered clear of him. He made them edgy, probably because they sensed he was not quite human, not quite beast.

So Jonah hurried home, went inside and shifted to human where he'd be better able to deal with any problematic wolf, or make friends if it was so inclined. Though he recognized this was wishful thinking more than a realistic possibility. Older wolves were suspicious creatures.

Jonah got dressed and, armed with a knife, waited outside the cave. Sure a wolf might attack a human, but only if it were rabid or mentally deranged, which was unlikely given this one's intelligence—he hadn't been able to give it the slip.

Jonah had once befriended a she-wolf pup with a broken leg and she'd become a pet. His one friend in recent times, Jonah thought rather grimly, but Eliza had abandoned him for a mate and the life of a wolf. Though she visited occasionally, usually in the summer, to show off her new pups.

Jonah blinked, shrugging off the memory as he became a little appalled at his eagerness to befriend this older male that was obviously healthy. Oh well. He was lonely. What was new about that?

He spent too much time alone so any encounter was welcome. Just accept that reality. As long as he was smart, it would be fine. He turned his knife blade up, touching its edge to bring the point home. Yeah, he wanted to greet the wolf, not kill it, but if killing somehow became a necessity, he knew what to do. He'd killed before.

He crouched in the doorway. At least the wind had faded here, and if he listened carefully, he could hear the creature approaching.

The snow was less deep, in this harbor against the elements. A clever place to make a den. Trey slowed right down and kept his ears open. Lynx were capable of moving silently, and Trey did not intend to be attacked without forewarning.

In the distance, he saw a small clearing, and he approached it cautiously. As he was about to reach its edge, a voice floated over the cold air, startling him.

"Hey, wolf." A rich tenor. Not old, but certainly not a boy's.

Trey went stock-still as a shiver thrilled through him. He'd anticipated a shifter, but somehow the reality of it was a shock. A giant-lynx shifter. *Amazing.*

His next thought followed swiftly—his employers could never, *ever* know. This was one more secret Trey intended to guard, because cat shifters were precious and rare, and this lynx shifter might be unique.

"I can hear you so you might as well come out. My hearing is quite good, as it happens."

The words were friendly, welcoming. The man-lynx was rational. Relief swept over Trey. He'd refused to think far ahead, past a potential attack, as he dreaded being forced to kill such a wonderful creature as this. He stepped forward a pace or two.

"You've been following me." The voice was clear, solid, clean. "That's okay, if we're going to be friends."

The lynx didn't yet recognize he was speaking to a fellow shifter. He thought Trey was an actual wolf. Which suggested he was inexperienced or uneducated.

Exactly how isolated was this lynx? Trey approached to find out.

A man crouched in a doorway to a...cave. Jesus, he lived in a cave. His body was loose, ready to move, but not aggressive in the least. Trey couldn't make out much beyond the layers of warm clothing, but the man seemed fairly large as he turned his gaze on Trey.

They stared at each other, assessing, the man frowning a little. His eyes—green—widened in his pale, well-shaven face. This one had not let himself go wild enough to grow a years-old beard, and he wore modern winter gear. Encouraging.

"I haven't been followed home before," he said softly. He cocked his head. "I'm not sure exactly what you seek here. I've got a knife and I'll use it to defend myself, but I really don't want to do that. You're a handsome fellow."

Well, it was good to know the shifter shared Trey's reluctance to attack. He realized that his own posture was aggressive. But this lynx was no werewolf who'd be looking to see if Trey was dominant or not, so Trey consciously relaxed his body. He stepped towards him, then stopped to utter a friendly greeting. It was a little annoying to act the wolf, but under the circumstances, necessary.

The lynx smiled and it was then, being closer and seeing that smile, that Trey realized how young he was. A strange disappointment ran through him, but he didn't stop to examine it because fast on its heels followed concern. One this young should not be on his own. It was hard on a shifter to balance human social needs and a cat's desire for solitude, and many couldn't handle their split personalities. Werewolves had an easier time integrating their two halves.

Trey peered, examining that face, assessing. Okay, this one was in his twenties, probably closer to twenty than thirty.

"Are you hungry?" The words broke Trey's train of thought and he sat, waited. He'd never been particularly vocal, but he allowed himself a brief guttural whine that the lynx took as a yes. "I'll bet. You've had a long day, following me like that." He frowned. "Though you sure don't look malnourished. I guess winter's been treating you well?"

Not really, but Trey didn't think he'd bother explaining how he was an FBI agent poised to infiltrate an unnamed agency full of assholes and murderers who would kill him if they ever found out he was a shifter. Even if he could speak, he wouldn't burden anyone with that information.

"Good." The lynx smiled again, a trusting expression that struck Trey as something like a gift. The young man patted his chest. "I'm Jonah, by the way." He looked beyond Trey. "And the storm is not going away yet. I think you'd better come in. Do I have to tempt you with food?" Jonah moved inward, holding open a makeshift door, so Trey pushed up from sitting and trotted past Jonah to go right inside.

He blinked. It was dark but spacious and it went deep. Not only that, there was a real, in a Home Depot sort of way, door inside. It led to a tiny house *inside* the cave. Into which Jonah disappeared, not inviting Trey this time.

Interesting. Trey wanted to see the house itself, not just this cave-like mudroom, but that could wait till Jonah was more at ease with him. Meanwhile, he took in all the smells, searching for the presence of any other creatures, human or not. He only identified the lynx shifter. Evidently Jonah lived alone and didn't have many visitors. Trey intended to ensure that Jonah didn't regret this one.

Jonah interrupted Trey's brief investigation of the mudroom by returning with a slab of raw deer meat. Not Trey's favorite meal, but it would do.

"What do you think?" Jonah sounded pleased with this gift of food. "It's been a while since I've had company." There was a wry note to his words, suggesting it was an understatement. Trey wondered just how lonely Jonah got. Older cat shifters sometimes gave up on humanity. But the younger ones still wanted to engage.

"Dig in. It's all yours." Jonah placed the platter of food halfway between Trey and himself, and Trey came forward. He hadn't realized he was hungry till he began eating. "Now, I have to make my meal, which takes a little more preparation since I prefer my stuff cooked. But we'll talk more later, okay?"

Jonah stepped into the little house again, shutting the door, and this time Trey didn't think he'd come out any time soon. Which was no good. Trey was absolutely fascinated by the young lynx. Even this house he lived in was fascinating. Who had built it for him, or had he made it himself? It was made of wood that no doubt kept the heat in and the beasts out.

Including Trey. But having made contact, Trey didn't intend to spend the night in this pseudo-porch, not quite inside, not outside. He wanted to listen to Jonah's young, earnest voice. His face had a raw-boned appeal, pale skin over high cheekbones, a wide mouth, big eyes. All softened by those freckles and that smile.

Jonah seemed sane, which suggested that he hadn't raised himself, that he'd been socialized. Certainly his English appeared perfectly normal.

The desire to shift grabbed hold of Trey. He wanted to shift and talk with the young man, find out his story, find out if he needed help. Not in the short term, as Jonah appeared quite self-sufficient. But how did he plan to manage long term on his own like this?

But it was not yet time for Trey to reveal himself. The wolf had gained some measure of Jonah's trust and Trey thought it wise to build on that before proceeding.

Interesting that Jonah still hadn't identified Trey as a fellow shifter. A lynx had an excellent sense of smell, almost as strong as a wolf's. Trey's best guess was that Jonah had not

16

encountered a shifter before and therefore had no experience in recognizing one. Trey might appear to be a strange-smelling wolf.

There was a handle on the door to the inner sanctum, so after eating, Trey left his empty platter and walked to the entrance to the real house. He raised his paw and carefully pushed down on the metal lever. The latch gave way, releasing the door from its frame, and he shouldered the door so it swung inward. Barking once in greeting, he moved in slowly, only to stop and stare, amazed at the presence of bookshelves and other furniture—a bed, a bench, a rug. In the midst of this snowstorm, it seemed almost magical.

Someone had a real home here, out in the middle of nowhere. No electricity—the lighting came from the fire and lanterns—but this was a home. He stared, and Jonah stared back at him, mouth slightly open in consternation.

"Well, that was some trick, opening that door. Very clever." Crouching, Jonah had turned away from the fire on which he was cooking meat and potatoes. There wasn't alarm in his voice, but some wariness. "I actually thought you would stay outside. That's a thick coat of fur you have. Besides, you're letting in all the cold air."

Trey turned around and shouldered the door shut, then faced Jonah, sitting. Best not to move too much until the human became accustomed to his wolf's presence.

The look on Jonah's face was incredulous. "Exactly how much of what I'm saying do you understand?"

Trey felt like laughing and managed a wolfish grin. But he made a mental note to himself not to overdo it and unnerve the lynx. Let Jonah get used to his wolf for a day or two, then break the news to him that he wasn't the only shifter in his own house.

Chapter Two

It particularly intrigued Jonah that the wolf was not young. Not old either. Rather, middle-aged. He informed his visitor of that fact and was rewarded by another of those wolfie grins. Eliza had given them out too, though not so easily.

But, back to his main puzzle. Younger wildlife were more likely to seek out companionship, less likely to be wary of humans. And this one wasn't injured and appeared to be in perfect health despite the cold winter. Maybe it was simply the snowstorm that had inspired this wolf to arrive on Jonah's doorstep, but wolves knew how to find shelter and didn't generally follow him home.

"You're an enigma," Jonah told him. "I think I'll name you that."

The wolf's ears pricked up.

"I'll have to tell you about the history of the Enigma machine if you hang around long enough. Bet you can't wait for that. It was important in World War II."

Those striking blue eyes—Jonah recalled that wolves had brownish eyes not blue—blinked at him as if he were an intriguing puzzle himself. At least Jonah hoped that's what that expression meant, and not that the wolf saw him as his next delicious meal.

Nah. For one thing, the wolf was fagged out, his head lying

on his paws after polishing off that slab of meat. As Jonah sat to eat his own meal, he realized the wolf might be thirsty. He poured some water in a bowl and set it between them.

Jonah wasn't stupid. He knew wild animals could be unpredictable. This one had already surprised him by tracking him home, and then having the gall and wherewithal to open his door. So Jonah kept his senses on alert and the knife within reach.

He wasn't sure what he was going to do about sleeping, to be honest, but that was a few hours away, and a few hours' observation would allow him to make a decision. God knows it was a relief to have something new and different to think about.

In the meantime he would talk to the creature who regarded him with such an intelligent gaze. As Jonah put water on the fire to boil, he said, "Hey, do you have some husky in you? That might explain why you're so friendly and why you have blue eyes."

Enigma lifted his head and his look of disdain had Jonah laughing out loud.

"What? Have you got something against huskies? They're nice dogs. Closely related to wolves, though yes, they are dogs."

In response, Enigma shook himself and returned to drinking. As Jonah's smile faded, he caught himself. He sure was reading a lot of emotion and understanding into that canine face. Gawd, he was obviously a little desperate. The anxiety that gripped him in the winter was never completely at bay and its claws tightened, briefly, just to let him know he was not free of it, despite the temporary reprieve that had come with this visitor. Yes, the wolf's gaze was intent, but after all, he'd fed it lovely meat. It was probably hoping for an encore, not understanding Jonah's every uttered word. And there were so many of them. Now that he'd started, he couldn't stop talking. He'd had no one to speak to for too long. His conversation turned inane.

"Did you know I have lynx-green eyes?" Jonah placed a finger at the outer corner of one eye, and Enigma's gaze tracked the motion. "So did my mother, not that she was a lynx herself, she only carried the genes and the eye color. Lynx green means muddy green. It's really ordinary hazel, but lynx green sounds more impressive, right? Besides there's a good reason I have these eyes." He rose to wash the dishes. The words continued though Jonah wished he could stop the flow, because he didn't actually *want* to speak of Craig, but he needed to. His throat thickened.

"My brother, on the other hand, had brown eyes, like his father." Jonah paused, the old pain still there. He hadn't talked about it to anyone but the baby rabbit he'd rescued. "My brother's dead, he froze to death. My fault."

There, his voice sounded calm. He wanted to be calm about it. He'd spent too much time in anguish over the past three years. He pulled in a long breath. "I've been a bit lonely since then, and guilty, so I wanted to confess. You seem like the confessor-type. Anyway I'm glad you've come, though I'm a little concerned about our sleeping arrangements tonight."

When he went silent, the preternatural wolf rose to his feet and walked closer. Jonah stiffened, thinking about the knife, though rather wearily. *Stay smart*, he admonished himself.

But the wolf just lay down closer to him. This was no attack dog.

Jonah wanted to say more, tell Enigma that Craig had been two years younger than him, that Craig had been too angry after their mother had disappeared, that at nineteen Craig had had little common sense. But Jonah bit down on his tongue. Craig deserved to rest in peace and not be criticized. The words would hang heavy on Jonah later if he did complain. Instead he talked about his library and the books he'd read recently, giving a précis of them while the wolf listened with great interest—or so it appeared.

A few hours passed like that, and Jonah actually found his voice beginning to falter, out of shape after being silent for too long. So they went out for a "restroom break". Jonah still liked saying that, even to Enigma. It had been his mother's euphemism. Craig had thought it more hilarious than it really was, but some of his humor had rubbed off on Jonah.

The wolf came back in, and Jonah made the decision to stop carrying the knife. If it was his fate to be killed by a split-personality wolf—because no way was this creature vicious, Jonah could practically smell its goodwill—then so be it. There were worse fates, and going quietly insane from loneliness and cold was one of them.

He extinguished the two lanterns, then stoked up the fire for the night before he lay on his cot. The wolf settled on the wool rug nearby, letting out a long, contented sigh.

"Good night to you too, Enigma."

It snorted in response, as if a name was not at all necessary, and Jonah grinned. For the first night in a long time the loneliness didn't threaten to trap him as he fell asleep. He was going to hold on to this companionship if it was at all possible.

He should have tried befriending healthy wildlife earlier, not only rescues. But his mother had always discouraged animal friendships, saying he needed to stay focused on his human. Besides, she'd argued, the smarter animals seemed to sense something strange about Jonah, his dual nature making them skittish, uneasy. But Enigma here didn't mind lynx shifters.

Rolling his eyes at himself and his expectations, Jonah admonished himself. Enjoy what it was for what it was. It didn't do to think too hard on the future. It never had.

21

The next morning Trey watched Jonah bustle around the small hut, making breakfast. There was light from the fire again, as the first thing Jonah did was remake it, but there also was some kind of natural skylight, a window in the roof of the hut and then a small patch of cloudy sky seen through a hole in the cave. Trey was impressed, by the structure, by the library, by Jonah's supplies.

His supplies were heavy on the meat, but fresh kills were not Jonah's only source of nourishment. Someone, maybe Jonah himself, had stocked this place with dried goods: flour, rice, beans and vitamins. And a large stash of vitamin C. Obviously Jonah didn't want to get scurvy and didn't know a lynx could make its own vitamin C, as could Trey.

Well, it was heartening to see that someone had cared for this young man enough to educate him, even if incorrectly in some details. Perhaps the dead brother Jonah had found painful to mention. His face had creased with pain right before he'd spoken of Craig.

Trey trotted into the back room, closet-sized, to discover clothing, most of it pretty modern. Along with high-tech winter camping gear. So did Jonah have some money, an inheritance? And how did he get hold of all this stuff when he seemed so alone?

These were all questions Trey wanted answers to. Not only was it his job to protect shifters of all shapes and sizes, he also liked to prevent problems from arising. A lonely lynx who went a little crazy with the solitude could lead to problems.

"Hey, what are you doing?" Jonah came back to see Trey's nose in his makeshift wardrobe, made of rough pine. "You have got to be the nosiest wolf ever. There *must* be some husky in you."

It was ridiculous to be annoyed by this accusation of being

part domesticated dog. Especially when tuft-haired, green-eyed Jonah was looking at him with such an open expression.

Jonah crouched beside Trey, all the lynx's caution of the previous night gone. "I've got this terrible desire to give you a pat. But I know it's unwise."

Yes.

"No matter how curious you are about my clothing, you're not a pet."

Goddamn right.

Besides if Jonah patted him, Trey was concerned he'd shift then and there. Under these circumstances, human touch would be a powerful inducement. He turned around and headed back to the fire.

"Have I offended you now? You're one strange beast. Okay, why don't I make amends by offering you breakfast?"

Trey licked his lips and Jonah eyed him.

"You know, I hope I'm not going stir-crazy here, because I swear you understand *exactly* what I'm saying, all the time."

Be careful. Trey didn't want to spook the lynx. Well, not yet. Shifting to human was going to shock Jonah. Trey decided he needed to withdraw a little and lay down quietly after breakfast, aiming for a low-key presence for at least a few hours.

They spent the rest of the day together, with Trey trying not to react to everything Jonah said and give away the depth of his understanding. The young man chatted volubly, as if he'd been deprived of the ability to speak. But he didn't mention his brother again, talked more about the weather and his concerns about how the deer might starve this winter, and about a semi-wild wolf named Eliza. His parents never came up, Trey noted, and he wondered what the story was there. In the afternoon, they briefly ventured out into the ongoing blizzard that was losing steam.

23

That evening, Jonah decided to read to "Enigma". Trey thought his new nickname a little ironic, given that he found Jonah to be exactly that. Jonah chose a nonfiction book, the history of math or some such. Trey didn't follow the words, apart from the fact that someone named Hilbert was apparently the last universal mathematician, but he enjoyed Jonah's voice. Later still, the lanterns were turned off, but a low fire continued to heat the place, and Jonah spoke to the ceiling.

"I'm glad you're here, Enigma. Getting snowed in, well, that's when I sometimes have a bad time of it."

Trey hadn't yet lain down, and the quiet way Jonah shared his feelings pushed Trey to show some level of affection. He lifted a paw and patted the sleeping bag that covered Jonah's legs. *I'm here*, he wanted to say. Not for long, but he was here, and he would keep in touch with this young man.

"My God, you have got to be the most empathetic creature I've ever known." But there was a smile in Jonah's voice. Trey had a terrible and wolf-like desire to lick Jonah's face, but he didn't think it fair when Jonah didn't truly know what he was. It felt too deceptive.

Bunching his pillow, Jonah turned on his side to face Trey. "Well, since you're such a good listener, maybe I should tell you." He paused, a kind of grimace crossing his face. "I've been thinking about my future, and I'm not actually sure how much longer I can last out here by myself."

Trey whined. *Crap.* He'd thought letting Jonah get used to Enigma first was a good idea, but maybe he needed Trey's human to talk to now.

"It's been three years since Craig died. I've run into some hikers in the summer and accosted them while they've stared at me like I'm a freak. But that's about it. When I'm in town, I'm too nervous to strike up much of a conversation. Too many people."

Fuck it. Trey nosed Jonah's arm. It had escaped the sleeping bag and he licked, liked the taste of salt and musk on young skin. He proceeded to lick Jonah's palm and fingers carefully and thoroughly while Jonah lay still, probably worried he'd scare Enigma away.

Then he rested his muzzle against Jonah's thick wrist.

He let out a long sigh. "Not that you can know, but I *am* a freak, that's the problem. I do manage to fetch supplies from town since they're essential, but I don't cope with crowds and strangers. It's a challenge to even buy something. That said, I'm not unhappy in the summer. Things look up and life is okay, not great but okay. Then winter comes again"—his voice cracked—"and I think I might go crazy."

There was silence for a while.

Jonah added, more softly, and he sounded more relaxed too, "So I'm glad you're here. You're helping. I can't believe how tame you are. Someone must have treated you well."

A strange, long-dormant ache pulsed in Trey's chest as a memory of Quinn surfaced. Quinn had, after all, treated Trey *very* well.

Blinking the memory away, he focused on the here and now, on the young man who, today, needed his company. Trey stayed by the cot and waited until Jonah's breathing changed to indicate he'd fallen asleep.

Then he circled around and lay down on the rug.

He slept lightly that night, waiting till near the end of Jonah's last deep-sleep cycle. As it started, Trey rose to see Jonah's face crease in pain again, as it had when he'd mentioned his dead brother, and Trey wanted to offer solace.

Now wasn't the time. He considered staying longer in wolf form, but two things concerned him. Jonah's loneliness, it was too strong to be healthy.

Also these confidences of Jonah's probably wouldn't have been voiced to a man he'd met twenty-four hours ago. If Trey remained Enigma longer and Jonah revealed more about himself, he might feel deceived, tricked, betrayed.

And Trey didn't want to sabotage what might be a difficult relationship with more of those one-sided confidences.

So he walked to the far side of the room, lay down and let go of his body. The world, already black since the fire had died, turned blacker as he bent his mind towards the shift, bending his body too when pain and oblivion overwhelmed him and he came close to passing out. Fur receded, bone and muscle stretched or contracted, and Trey bit back on a groan as he went under.

He woke heated by the shift. His alarm threatened to spike while he grimly tamped it down. *Assess the danger.* He rolled from his side onto his stomach and pushed up on all fours, being careful to stay silent in this strange place. As the idea that he'd been somehow kidnapped began to form, memory pushed itself forward and he recalled that he'd chosen to enter the house of...a lynx.

Trey shook his head and sat back on his haunches, letting the events of the past two days rush through him: Jonah, blizzard, cave.

It amazed him anew that he'd found a shapeshifting lynx, and a giant one at that. How incredibly rare.

This one had to be protected. At all costs.

Trey listened, intent on hearing Jonah whose breaths still indicated sleep, though perhaps not as deep as before. Trey walked silently to the wardrobe. At the very least he needed to pull on some pants. Jonah was only an inch or two shorter than him, and something in this wardrobe would fit Trey well enough. The clothing would offer some modesty, which might help with Jonah's coming shock and give Trey some warmth

26

after the initial flush of heat from shifting receded.

Trey pulled on long underwear that didn't reach his ankles. Then he shrugged on Jonah's jacket. In a basket he found socks—one of those expensive wool blends. Necessary on the now-frigid floor.

As a precaution, Trey returned to the main area and hid the knife Jonah had left by the fire. If the lynx panicked, Trey would rather they didn't end up grappling with that sharp blade.

He sat on a bench near the dead fire, facing Jonah's cot, and waited for the lynx to wake.

The sleeping Jonah sensed something was off and he stirred, frowning, pulling in a breath, trying to smell what was wrong. While he fought his way to consciousness, Trey worked to project calm.

Jonah rolled from his back onto his side to face Trey. Slowly he raised his eyelids, his gaze not yet focused.

He blinked, slight puzzlement only, because he wasn't yet awake. Then he closed his eyes again, stiffened, and his eyes flew open. Jonah flinched in fear. Not good.

"Hello," Trey offered. At first Jonah seemed paralyzed and though Trey wasn't used to doling out apologies, he thought one was owed here. "I'm sorry to startle—"

Jonah leapt out of the sleeping bag, almost tripping as he extracted his legs, and then he was off the cot and into the corner beside it. He grabbed a piece of wood, and Trey, smelling a wave of terror flowing off him, thought, *shit*. He lifted his hands in surrender, palms out. "It's okay—"

Jonah threw the wood. Ducking, Trey shouted, "Jonah!" and that stayed Jonah's hand though he'd already picked up his next piece of wood. He remained silent, jaw clenched. His gaze darted about, probably looking for his knife.

Trey rose, backing up to give Jonah space. "I'm a friend." He kept the words as steady as possible. Someone human had hurt the lynx.

"Get. Out." The words were close to growls, low and terse to mask the fact that Jonah's voice shook. Trey breathed in anger, and fear.

Jonah threw the second piece of wood and Trey caught it easily. "Jonah, *think.*"

He cowered. Okay, wrong thing to say as Trey watched him reach for another piece of firewood and whip it at Trey. Again he caught it with two hands, let it drop to the floor.

Jonah scrabbled for more and Trey, with two strides, was upon him. It wasn't how he'd wanted this first meeting to go and Jonah was strong, going after him with teeth and hands and feet. But Trey had practice in this, long practice, and he easily wrestled Jonah stomach-down, hands behind his back, Trey's weight on him without hurting him.

"Jonah, I need you to calm down."

The lynx's breathing rasped in and out, and Trey could hear the too-rapid heartbeat. He no longer knew how to communicate with this man, though they were now both human.

Chapter Three

"I am not here to hurt you."

Fuck you. Aaron always talked as if he didn't intend to hurt him. It was such *bullshit.* And when he didn't hit Jonah, Aaron hit Craig or his mother instead.

"Jonah."

It was the same as always, Aaron making him completely helpless before the beating began. Jonah pulled in a huge breath, preparing to fight again, and...

What the fuck? He was losing it. He wasn't at the old house. Craig wasn't here. *This isn't even Aaron.*

Jonah couldn't breathe. Aaron wasn't here, but the panic was.

"It's okay."

No it wasn't okay. They were all dead, dead, dead.

A hand went to Jonah's temple, palm smoothing his hair back. Very strange. Weirdly calming.

He could only conclude that he'd finally snapped.

"Jonah." A stranger's voice, and then the stranger stepped away. Jonah wasn't sure what to do. Aaron would have already informed him he couldn't move. But Aaron was *dead.*

After a moment, Jonah rolled onto his side. Nothing happened. He took a breath and launched himself to standing.

"Let's not start again, okay?" said the stranger.

Jonah could barely think straight. There was a large man in his room, staring at him and taking yet another step back. Jonah remembered to breathe and smelled...he smelled the wolf. Sort of.

He decided he'd better start listening to the words, because the stranger was speaking, his mouth was moving, but Jonah wasn't able to understand much beyond his name, not with the loud buzzing in his ears. He could *not* pass out. He focused, narrowed his eyes, became determined to get himself under control, and the buzzing receded enough for the words to make their way through.

"I'm sorry, Jonah."

How the hell did this asshole know his name? Something was desperately wrong. Aaron had betrayed them again. From beyond the grave? Was it possible?

"Sit down." The stranger gestured to the cot. "You're white as a sheet." The invader hunkered down on his own haunches, as if to demonstrate how one lowered one's body.

Jonah considered the advice and sank back onto the bed. Better than crashing to the floor unconscious.

"Breathe, Jonah." Like a puppet Jonah obeyed, dragging in needed breaths, trying to stave off the lightheadedness and the godawful buzzing. Why did he smell Enigma and not see him? Was the wolf okay?

"Look at me."

Not yet. Jonah clenched his fists, stared down and tried to get his head together, though it was still full of Aaron, despite the stranger's presence.

"Jonah." The word was soft, coaxing, and before this morning, it had been such a long while since anyone had said his name aloud. He couldn't resist, and reluctantly Jonah met the stranger's blue *familiar* gaze. How could anyone be familiar?

"You know my name?" The words were high and thin, and the question stupid. Obviously this guy knew his name. He'd said it repeatedly since Jonah had awakened. Embarrassment heated his face.

The stranger didn't use his weakness against him, didn't laugh. His expression was concerned, sympathetic and, perhaps most unsettling, showed intense interest. "You told me your name."

Jonah didn't remember that, which was too scary to understand. He latched on to something else. "Where's Enigma? Is he okay?"

The man simply stared—with Enigma's brilliant eyes—and Jonah felt the blood draining from his brain again.

"Jonah." He had told Enigma his name, introduced himself, but a wolf turning into a man...? Impossible. Such a thing didn't exist. Despite all his efforts to keep it together, Jonah slumped over.

Trey slid forward, catching Jonah before he hit the floor, then lifted him back on the cot. He was out for less than a minute while Trey gazed down, rather guiltily, at the white face that made the freckles stand out in dark relief.

Jonah's eyelids fluttered open and Trey hoped *this* awakening went a little more smoothly than the first. It couldn't get worse, he didn't think. Then Jonah flinched. Christ. Trey did not want an unending loop of this panicked reaction, and as painful as it was for him to watch, Jonah was having a harder time living through it.

So Trey backed up. He'd thought talking to Jonah would help matters, but words—especially his name—seemed to come as a shock, with his eyes widening every time Trey uttered it.

Perhaps because he'd spent so much time alone. Trey could remember coming back from a stint in the wilderness and getting used to listening to conversation again. This time, Trey went back down on his haunches about six feet away from the bed. Looming over Jonah had already sent the lynx into attack mode once.

Rather shakily, Jonah pushed himself up to sitting.

Don't stand, implored Trey silently. *You would have cracked your head on the floor if I hadn't caught you two minutes ago.*

The fear was still there in Jonah's scent, but not as overwhelming. Very little color seeped back into his cheeks.

He sat back to lean against the wall and scrubbed his face. Again, he looked around the room, probably in search of Trey's wolf, before his gaze landed on Trey.

"What..." He swallowed hard. "How'd you find me?"

Trey wasn't sure who Jonah thought he was, and though a little reluctant to drop—again—the bomb of being Enigma, Trey thought it important to bring some understanding of the situation to Jonah.

"Do my eyes look familiar?"

Jonah frowned, in some distress. "I'm the only one."

"Only shifter?"

Jonah's gaze skittered away.

"You're not. I'm a shifter. You may be the only lynx shifter. Wolves are more common." He kept his voice matter-of-fact and though he wanted to say more, explain everything, talk about the giant-lynx report, he kept his mouth shut and waited for Jonah to ask another question. Jonah hadn't been spoken to, perhaps for years, though Trey hoped for Jonah's sake it hadn't been that long. It would take him more than half an hour to get used to having a conversation that wasn't one-sided.

"Who told you about me?" Jonah demanded.

"No one." At the patent disbelief on Jonah's face, Trey added, "I smelled you. Shifters have a particular scent. Perhaps you've noticed that about me." Trey patted his chest, mirroring Jonah's action of two days ago. "I'm Enigma. You'll remember my 'husky' eyes. You'll smell that I'm a wolf."

Jonah stared and Trey watched for his face to go white again, but instead it flushed. The poor guy was easily embarrassed, but if it drew blood to his head, Trey figured it was better than not being embarrassed.

"I'm sorry I've startled you. That wasn't my intention."

Jonah looked away and back again, his expression doubtful.

"I knew it would be a surprise," Trey amended. "But I'd hoped that meeting a fellow shifter might be something worthwhile for you. I have found it can be a relief to talk with someone where you don't have to hide your other half, or explain it."

"Worthwhile." There was a kind of dullness to the word.

Trey grimaced. "I'm not explaining myself very well. But since I realized what you were, I've been excited about meeting you."

"Excited." He said the word as if it made no sense, and after a moment of examining its meaning, he gave up. "How did you find me?"

This seemed to be a big concern of the lynx and Trey's interest sharpened. "Are you worried someone is looking for you?"

"Not now. I've made that impossible." Jonah eyed him. "I thought."

"I think you're difficult to find. This was mostly luck."

"Mostly?"

"There has been a report of a giant lynx. You're quite large."

Jonah actually rolled his eyes, which Trey took as progress. A reaction instead of the dull repetition of one of Trey's words. "That's hardly the most unusual thing about me. You're as big as I am."

Trey nodded to acknowledge both these facts. He was a big wolf.

"You're Enigma?" Jonah blurted out.

"Trey, actually. But you called me Enigma and fed me a slab of deer meat the first night. You described me as a handsome fellow." Here Trey offered a small grin, but Jonah didn't react. He simply looked dumbfounded. "You don't believe in werewolves? Despite the fact you're a cat shifter?" He supposed if he'd been isolated from all shifters all his life, it might not be easy to believe.

"I'm a *mutant.*"

Trey lifted an eyebrow at that. "I doubt it."

"Are there others?"

"Why don't we have breakfast and then talk some more?"

"God, I can't eat. I feel like I'm going to throw up." He cast Trey a look, like he shouldn't have admitted that weakness.

"I'm sorry. That's not my usual effect on people, but I understand this meeting has been unusual."

Jonah hunched, as if the joke was on him. "I'm not used to people being in my home."

"I know," Trey said quietly. "You told me."

Again Jonah's face flushed.

"That's nothing to be embarrassed about. You've done amazingly well."

"At what?" he demanded, for the first time sounding

aggressive.

"Setting yourself up here." Trey gestured to the hut and its furnishings.

"Don't make fun of me," Jonah said stiffly.

"No. I wouldn't. I'm too impressed."

It took Jonah about half a minute to decide that either Trey was sincere or it wasn't worth challenging him on it. "If you shifted, you must be starving."

"I am."

Slowly Jonah slid off the bed, edged around Trey who remained low to the ground, and pulled on his winter coat. "I'll make breakfast in a moment."

Outside it was frigid. The storm was finally over and with the blue sky came plummeting temperatures. Jonah could only indulge in a few minutes away from the intruder before his skin started to freeze. Not that he was in any shape for an outing, not when he felt like he'd been run over by a Mack truck. Between flashing back to Aaron and coping with actually talking to someone and, most embarrassingly, fainting, Jonah was only going on nerves and leftover adrenaline.

He ducked back into the cave, though not into the house itself yet. Blowing on his hands, he tried to wrap his head around the astonishing events of this morning. He'd gone to bed with a wolf in his room and woken in the company of a strange man who claimed to be a shifter. Well, a werewolf.

Jonah believed in himself, because he had no choice, but it was hard to believe in another. His mother had claimed they were unique, her line of mutant lynx shifters. She'd claimed they had to hide from everyone.

Well, Jonah hadn't quite succeeded and he wasn't sure what he thought about it.

Okay, he'd longed for company, daydreamed about meeting a fellow hermit who wanted to befriend him, who could be trusted. The yearning had sometimes been intense but had not prepared him for the reality of this stranger. What was he supposed to do? Whether Jonah trusted the wolf or not was irrelevant. The man *knew*. On top of that, Jonah could barely think with another human in the room with him, watching him. It felt invasive and this situation had nothing to do with the affable fantasy companions of his imagination.

And yet, despite his intense discomfort, he had so many questions to ask. While Jonah didn't want the man around, he dreaded the idea of Enigma or Trey actually leaving before Jonah had the chance to learn more about a fellow shifter. A window had opened up, an intense, uncomfortable window, but he didn't want it closed yet. He'd thought he was completely alone in this dual world of his, and it looked like he'd been wrong.

If only he could get Aaron out of his head, it might be easier. He might not have freaked out to such an extent. That he'd thought Aaron had risen from the grave and found him was something else indeed.

Jonah let out a long, shuddery breath. Aaron was dead, he reminded himself. And who knew better than he. Six years ago, after his mother was gone, Jonah had turned lynx, stalked his mother's ex-boyfriend and ripped out Aaron's throat. Cold-blooded murder. Jonah didn't regret the killing and never would.

Chapter Four

Trey could hear Jonah pacing in the cave outside the door, but the lynx didn't return to the warm inner room. Was he going to have to coax the cat back inside?

He counted to fifty then moved towards the door. Jonah probably heard his steps because the door swung inwards before Trey reached it.

They both froze. Trey because he didn't wish to startle Jonah again, and Jonah because he appeared to regard Trey as the enemy. Trey backed up and once again lowered himself, this time next to the fire he'd started.

The cat shivered and slipped in, shutting the door behind him.

"Come warm up." Trey swept an arm towards the burgeoning flames.

"I'm fine." Jonah shoved his hands under his armpits and looked for all the world like he didn't belong in his own home, which was not what Trey wanted at all.

"Do you mind if I make us some porridge?"

Jonah simply shrugged, the gesture stiff, his expression suspicious.

All right. Porridge it was. Silently, Trey found the pot and the oatmeal, boiled some water and served out two bowls. He'd observed how the kitchen area was arranged yesterday so it wasn't difficult to get what they needed.

He backed away from the fire and left Jonah's bowl near it, hoping the lynx would move towards warmth because he wasn't doing a good job of hiding the tremors running through his body.

When Trey was about halfway through his bowl, Jonah approached the fire, picked up his portion of porridge and gulped it down so that he was finished at the same time as Trey. Jonah proceeded to provide them with water and beef jerky, then washed the dishes. Trey's offer of help was received with a shake of the head.

When Jonah finished his chores, he turned and looked startled to see Trey had hunkered down on the thick wool rug where he'd slept the night before, or perhaps he was just startled to see Trey. It might take more than an hour to get used to the idea of a visitor if you never had them. Trey wanted to tell the cat to sit and relax, but the only place to sit, besides the makeshift bench which Jonah had lowered himself onto, was the cot. Right now, Trey was blocking the way to the cot.

Trey scratched his beard, briefly wondering if he'd be able to borrow shaving supplies in the future, then turned his mind back to the matter at hand. The truth was, he was used to taking charge, laying out orders and being the tactician. He was widely regarded as cold and he liked it that way. But here he'd stumbled upon a young man who needed to be coaxed into at least a minimal amount of trust.

He couldn't remember the last time he'd made connections with anyone. He just did his job.

"What do you want from me?" Jonah was staring at the dying fire. It needed to be built up again and, indeed, the young man crouched down and poked before adding a couple more logs.

There was a large pile of wood in the cave. He would've had

to spend a lot of time cutting up trees. While it wasn't a full-time job to live like this through the winter, it quite definitely took some effort, some forethought.

When Trey didn't answer, Jonah glanced up, a mutinous expression on his face, like he wasn't going to repeat himself. So Trey considered the question. What *did* he want from Jonah?

"I don't want anything," he began carefully.

"Then why are you here?"

"Would you prefer I leave?"

Jonah shrugged, which Trey found interesting. Good. Perhaps there was some curiosity to carry them past this awkward introduction.

He tried to start again, though honest to God, conversation had never come easily to him. "I was on vacation—"

"You work?" This asked in a tone that suggested Trey had accomplished the impossible.

"Yes."

"What's your job?" There was a kind of eagerness there, muted by Jonah's suspicions, but Trey responded to Jonah's desire for knowledge. He wondered how much Jonah knew or didn't know about the outside world.

"Law enforcement." Trey was not going to get more specific than that.

"So, you're like police."

"Yes." He wasn't police, but *like police* was close enough.

Jonah poked the fire again, making it unnecessarily smoky. "Do they know? Do the people you work with know you're a werewolf?"

"No." His handler, Kingley, suspected something was going on and was dangerously curious about Trey, but he was trying to fix that.

"Does anyone know?"

"Well, you do."

This brought Jonah around to face him. His eyes were fire-lit green, his face pale with red splotches, perhaps from the heat of the fire, perhaps from his obvious stress.

"Who knows about you, Jonah?" Trey asked.

"Just you," he mumbled, voice low.

"Where's your family?"

"Dead." Jonah probably wasn't aware of the bruised expression that crossed his face when he uttered that one word. "Where's your family?"

Fair enough. Jonah had questions and Trey tried to answer them, even if he didn't want to. "My parents are dead. I have a daughter I never see. Not werewolf."

"Oh." Jonah's brow furrowed, but he didn't ask for more information on her. "No brothers or sisters?"

Trey said heavily, "I have a younger brother."

"Is he a werewolf too?"

"Yes. But we're not close." It was hard to talk about Gabriel, and Jonah must have noticed because he wore a slight frown.

"My brother wasn't a lynx."

"I'm sorry that he's gone."

Jonah accepted that with a sharp nod. But he didn't let go of his interest in Gabriel. "Do you see your brother?"

"No." Trey shook his head, saw that Jonah was expecting more, and Trey weighed his options. If he shut down, Jonah would shut down, that seemed pretty evident. "My brother is...unstable, and hates me."

"Unstable."

There was no sense dancing around it, although a stone settled in Trey's chest, as it always did when he thought about Gabriel. "He's a killer."

"You're not?"

"I'm not unstable." This wasn't quite the way Trey had wanted the conversation to go. Except the comment didn't alarm Jonah. In fact his gaze intensified.

"Not all killers are unstable." It was a statement. Kind of. He also wanted validation.

"That is my belief." Trey tucked away Jonah's comment for later and tried to steer the conversation elsewhere. "I was on vacation..."

He waited, in case Jonah had something else to say or ask, but Jonah just nodded encouragement.

"I like to be alone on vacation, to be wolf." If it had been anyone else besides this young man who managed to be wary and yet eager, Trey would have felt stupid for sounding so awkward. But he supposed Jonah might not have had many people in his life to compare him to. So his conversational skills didn't have to be strong, as long as he communicated *something*. "But I need some kind of purpose when I'm on vacation, or I'm too much at loose ends."

Here, Jonah nodded again, almost fiercely.

"So I'd heard of a giant-lynx sighting and I thought I'd check it out."

Fear entered Jonah's expression. "Will there be others looking for me?"

"I doubt it. Though I'd be careful not to run into any more humans, at least when you're lynx. I assumed I was off on a wild-goose chase."

"What if I'd just been a giant lynx?"

"I would have found that interesting." Trey offered a half-smile. "But you're more interesting."

Jonah flushed, which wasn't what Trey had been aiming for. He had to try not to embarrass his host.

Pulling a breath in, Jonah stood. "The deer may starve."

Huh? "What?"

"After this kind of blizzard, with this much snow, the deer may starve."

Undoubtedly true, but this wasn't something Trey had given any thought to.

"So I'm going to cut down a few trees for them and they can eat. What's left can become firewood."

"All right." It had been enough talking as far as Trey was concerned too. At least for now. "How many will you feed?"

"Some," Jonah said shortly. He marched back to pull on warm gear from head to toe, then reappeared to say, rather defiantly, "I'm not stupid. I know it won't save them all. But it's okay to save a few."

"Sure." Frankly, Trey had never considered deer and their survival, except when he had to eat.

"I hate seeing them starve. It's better to kill them than that." He paused. "I don't have winter gear for you to wear. Craig's stuff is still here, but it's too small."

"I can shift."

Jonah straightened. "You leaving then?"

Trey kept the smile off his face. That wasn't anticipation, but dismay in Jonah's expression. Yes, the lynx was restless and uncomfortable sharing his space with Trey. But he didn't entirely want Trey to leave either. *Good.* "No, I'll follow you in a bit."

Looking down, Jonah placed hands on his hips. "I don't

usually hunt this herd."

"Okay," Trey said reasonably, "I won't hunt them either then."

"I've got enough food to feed us both. You don't have to take down a deer."

"Unless it's starving."

"Yeah, exactly." Jonah raised his gaze and stared at Trey. "I still don't know why you're here."

"When I figure it out, I'll let you know."

"Did you ever meet someone called Aaron Smythe?"

"Nope."

Jonah searched Trey's face, as if looking for truth. His eyes were wide and green, flecks of brown. Trey knew he shouldn't see this face as epitomizing innocence, knew that kind of thinking left him vulnerable even if it wasn't accurate. But it was hard to resist idealizing this young, isolated man.

Trey cleared his throat, returned to the question of Aaron Smythe. "Who is he?"

"He was my mother's boyfriend. For a couple of years."

"Craig's father?"

"No," said Jonah as if that was the end of it.

And for now, Trey let it be while noting that Jonah's mother had had at least three men in her life, and the last one had hurt Jonah. Trey intended to look up Aaron Smythe when he got back. "My coming here has nothing to do with him."

Jonah didn't exactly accept that, but he let it go. He tilted his head towards the door. "See you outside then."

Trey watched him leave, the door closing behind Jonah, his footsteps echoing until they hit the snow. Well, it had been a rough start, but not terrible, all things considered. To think he'd been worried to find a vicious, feral lynx shifter that had to be destroyed. Destroying feral shifters—and it had only been a handful—was the worst thing Trey had ever had to do.

But this was a lynx shifter who went out to feed the deer so they wouldn't starve to death. Trey had to smile to himself.

As soon as he shut the door behind him, Jonah let out a breath of relief. It had been intense, talking like that to a stranger, telling him his family was dead. It might have been unwise. Probably Jonah should have kept it vague, but at least Trey had answered about his own family. That made it feel less dangerous somehow.

Of course, Trey could be lying through his teeth and Jonah would never know. Irritably, he gave himself a shake and put on snowshoes. Not exactly the same as his paws, despite the description people sometimes gave of the lynx having snowshoe feet, but they would help keep him from sinking into the snow.

He set off for the cedar grove.

The deer steered clear of him, which suited Jonah fine. No sense taming deer and have them sitting ducks for hunters. They didn't deserve to have their edge of fear worn off because Jonah helped them out once in a while.

The only deer he'd ever half-tamed was the fawn he'd splinted a leg for. That little guy had got himself shot the following year, and while many deer got shot, Jonah felt guilty about it. So, yeah, that was the end of deer pets.

After he felled the first tree, Trey appeared. As wolf. Somehow this form made Jonah feel a lot more comfortable. While he *knew* Trey and Enigma were one and the same, the proof was reassuring.

But he said, "You shouldn't have come here."

Trey looked up at him, solemn and blue eyed.

Wiping the sweat from his face, Jonah added, "Your scent

is going to scare the deer away."

Trey jerked his head up towards Jonah.

"They're used to my scent."

Trey turned around and headed back, and Jonah felt a pang, perhaps a momentary panic.

"Wait," he shouted and Trey stopped. "I'm almost done, then we can leave together."

He felt stupid now, but Trey just settled on his haunches and waited him out. So Jonah resumed his work on the second tree, the ax slicing away more and more of the trunk until he could push the tree over.

"That'll do it." Gripping the ax, he walked towards Trey and suddenly felt at a loss, not used to explaining himself and his routine to anyone. He pointed to his right. "I, uh, usually walk this circuit. Partly because I can't stay inside all day and partly because it's got a good view, especially after a snowfall. But you don't have to come. I just ask you stay away from the cedars I cut down, so the deer can eat."

Trey probably thought it was strange to be concerned about deer, given that they both hunted and ate them. But Jonah had particular rules about what and who he killed, and the rules were important to him.

It took a good hour to walk up and around the path, as it always did, but the long view down from the ridge made Jonah feel better, and Trey-the-wolf seemed to appreciate it as well.

"It's best in winter. Once the leaves arrive in spring, the view gets cut off by the trees. Nice in the fall too though." He glanced to see if Trey was listening and Trey gave a low bark of acknowledgment. That made Jonah smile. He kind of wished Trey had stayed wolf. Then again, there was something to be said about having company that could talk back, no matter how stressful and alien it felt.

Not that he was ready for Trey to be human again, at least not immediately. As if he knew, that entire day Trey didn't shift. When Jonah bedded down for the night and the fire began to die, he finally asked, "What are you going to be when I wake up tomorrow?"

Trey looked up from the rug.

"Human?"

He gave an unwolflike nod.

Jonah swallowed. He could handle it. "Okay. I'll try not to be so alarmed this time."

It was supposed to be a joke, but he didn't hit quite the right note.

Then Trey did something odd. He rose and leaned against the cot. Jonah wasn't entirely sure of the message, but he imagined he was supposed to feel reassured.

His arm seemed to move of its own volition. Craig and he used to wrestle a lot when they were young; his mother had been affectionate. Still, Jonah had never touched a shifter. Tentatively he gave the top of Trey's head one awkward pat.

"Well. Good night, then."

Trey circled around and settled down on the rug again. It took Jonah longer than he liked to fall asleep, and he couldn't figure out if he was dreading or looking forward to tomorrow morning.

Chapter Five

Jonah woke with a start, sucking in air. Something was different. He blinked awake, taking in the sight of the strange man before him.

"Take it easy." Mere feet away, Trey crouched down, arranging wood for the morning fire.

Jonah tried to wrap his mind around there being a person in his home after three years on his own.

"Remember me?"

"Yes," Jonah snapped before he recognized Trey wasn't entirely serious. There was a wry quirk to his lips. "I mean," he added sheepishly, "of course."

Which sounded stupider and Jonah's face heated. It felt crowded in here, even if Trey was trying to give him space. After Jonah's performance yesterday, maybe Trey was worried that standing up would set him off.

"Relax," said Trey, lighting a match. "You've been on your own for a long time. It must be odd for you to have company, and uninvited company at that."

"What, are you a mind reader?"

"No psychic powers for me. But, and this isn't a bad thing"—the paper caught fire—"you wear your emotions on your face."

"I have to piss. Is that obvious too?"

"Only if you start hopping from foot to foot."

Jonah grabbed his warm clothes and headed outside. By the time he was back in, the fire was heating up the place. It was rather nice, not having to make fire in the frigid cold.

He looked down at Trey.

"You need better clothing if you ever go outside," Jonah observed.

Trey had on Jonah's inside clothes—long johns, socks, sweater, all a bit too tight and short. They revealed a powerful body. Those arms and shoulders were big and muscled, which made Jonah nervous. He'd already been tackled by Trey once. Granted, Jonah didn't plan on throwing wood at Trey again.

He glanced up. "I thought I'd stay in today."

Jonah shrugged. He didn't care. Much. "Do what you want."

"I'm tired from all the shifting, to be honest." This admission was a bit of a relief for Jonah to hear, given that Trey appeared to be so strong and all-round capable. A shapeshifter who lived in the real world with a job, who could track down other shifters like himself.

"I don't think I could do it. You went from wolf to human to wolf yesterday. And back to human this morning."

"I have good control. I need that for my work."

Jonah didn't know if he had good control or not, had nothing to gauge it by. He'd never thought about it much.

"I'm also starving."

With that Jonah pulled out the food, getting some meat this time, and they spent the next hour cooking, eating and cleaning up. Once they were both sated—Jonah's extra hunger seemed to have come from the surprise appearance of a werewolf yesterday—he sat on his cot and stared at Trey. He found he wanted to say something into the silence.

Jonah pitched his voice low to hide his uncertainty. "I still don't know why you're here, not really."

He kept asking this question, but if he could get a bead on Trey's motivation, he'd be better able to cope with what was coming next. Right now, everything seemed utterly unpredictable.

Lounging on the rug, Trey gazed at him through heavy eyelids. It had a weird effect on him. Jonah knew Trey looked like that because he was very full and very tired from yesterday's shifts, but his regard made Jonah feel strange, edgy.

"I'm here because you interest me."

The words felt like a compliment and embarrassed him. "So if I was dull, you'd be gone."

Trey's mouth kicked up, not really a smile, but amusement there. "Jonah."

He shivered a little, having someone call him by his name. Yes, Trey had said his name yesterday, but that was when Jonah had been in shock.

"You can't be dull. If you weren't a shifter, your hermit woodsman lifestyle would interest me."

"Oh."

"There aren't too many people who live as you do."

"I didn't exactly choose this."

Trey's eyelids lifted as he regarded Jonah seriously. "Who did?"

My mother. But that sounded immature, and Mom was long dead, so obviously he'd been making choices since then. "I mean, I didn't choose to be a lynx."

And then they'd had to hide from Aaron. Not that that had worked in the long run. But Jonah couldn't speak the truth about Aaron when Trey was police and would probably frown upon such matters as stalking and cold-blooded murder. That had to remain Jonah's secret.

"Of course not. You were born lynx," said Trey, and before Jonah could decide that was patronizing, he added, "We all have to work with what we're given." He paused. "Did someone threaten you?"

Jonah pulled on his outdoor gear while Trey lounged there on the floor. This morning, he'd been careful not to stand up, as if Jonah would freak out if Trey rose to his full height. The idea Trey had to tiptoe around him was getting on Jonah's nerves, or maybe just having Trey around was getting on his nerves.

Jonah needed some space. "I'm going outside for a while."

"Okay."

"You can use the cot if you want to sleep."

"Thank you." Trey sounded sincere. Then he leaned forward, placing a powerful arm across both his knees. The muscles on his forearm flexed under the thin material. It was mesmerizing. "Listen, Jonah."

Jonah pulled his gaze away from Trey's body and braced himself, though he didn't know for what. It was so strange conversing with someone, never knowing what they might talk about next, all the while getting distracted by any kind of movement. Craig and his mother had always been pretty predictable with what they had to say and how they moved, but Jonah knew virtually nothing about this guy.

"If you're finding it a little crowded here, I can come and go. I had intended to spend this vacation as wolf, so I don't mind being one, at all. But, I'd appreciate it if I could visit with you a little longer." The tone of Trey's voice was earnest.

Jonah felt his face redden. Again. He felt like he spent ninety percent of the time with Trey with a red face. He found himself looking at the ground.

"I just want to go out. Doesn't mean you have to go anywhere." With that, he took off, and hoped Trey would still be there when he returned.

Trey spent most of the day eating and sleeping, using that time to figure out his best course of action. What he really wanted to do was interrogate the younger man. Okay, mostly he wanted the results, all the answers that would explain Jonah and his existence to him. But Trey would have to be a little less heavy-handed than FBI. No sitting across the table with a one-way mirror and people looking in.

Even in that situation, it was often necessary to establish some kind of rapport, no matter how limited and temporary. Here and now, Trey needed to win the confidence of a skittish lynx with a charming propensity for blushing. Good thing Jonah was young and untried, or Trey's interest might have turned sexual, and he didn't have the strength to deal with that complication now.

When the lynx returned in the late afternoon, Trey heard him in the cave first. He could almost imagine Jonah working up his nerve to enter his inner sanctum, which had been invaded by a wolf. Then and there, he decided that tomorrow he'd give Jonah a break from company, allow him a couple of days to himself before he returned.

Besides, if Jonah was as lonely as it seemed, Trey's absence might be a way to make him look forward to having company instead of dreading it. A bit manipulative maybe, but not a terrible approach.

That evening went quietly, with Jonah not particularly talkative and Trey not insisting on conversation. His talking made Jonah edgy. But as they were getting ready for bed, he said, "I'll head out tomorrow."

Jonah's head jerked up. He'd been sitting by the fire, absorbing the heat after a day out in the bitter cold. He didn't say anything, just looked on full alert, shoulders stiff, face wary. Something a little tender loosened in Trey's chest at the young man's reaction, something Trey hadn't felt for a long time. *Be careful*, he warned himself.

Trey continued casually, "I'd like to see what lies farther up the ridge. I thought I'd go for a couple of days, as wolf, and then return." Here was the zinger. "If that's okay with you."

He'd been too long on the job to look like he was holding his breath or felt any kind of suspense in waiting for Jonah's reaction. The lynx was clearly torn by his need for company and his desire to be alone.

He turned back to the fire and poked, shoulders relaxing a fraction. "Sure. Fine with me."

The words were terse, but Trey sensed relief there.

Okay, good. And maybe after two days' absence, Jonah would find his presence less burdensome. If nothing else, the cat needed to wrap his head around the idea that he had a visiting werewolf. After three years of no company, it had to be something of a jolt.

Before Jonah woke the next morning, Trey was gone, having shifted some time during the night. Jonah rose alone, lit the fire, ate breakfast and got dressed to go out. No conversation was required, which was easier, but loneliness and its claws were quick to grab on to him.

Was Trey the kind of guy to keep his word and return? It

struck Jonah that way, but he didn't have a lot of experience in judging character. For now, though, he had chores to do.

The deer would have eaten bare the trees he'd cut down for them, so he could go chop up that cedar for firewood. While not the best firewood in the world—it burned too fast—he quite liked the smell.

It took him the better part of a day to work on the trees and haul the wood back home. The following day he chose to spend inside, given that Trey might be returning at which point Jonah would be made restless by another's presence in his small home. He also toyed with the idea of trying to find Trey, who didn't seem like the kind of guy to give warnings to, but the snow was treacherous here after a heavy fall.

Jonah had come across his brother frozen to death, and he didn't want to ever find someone else like that again.

He gave himself a shake and settled down to read and study. As usual, Craig's semi-jeering yet brotherly *Studying for what?* echoed in his head, and this time Jonah smiled at the memory. Craig had been a bright kid, but too active to apply himself to any kind of homework. It had made homeschooling a difficult proposition for his mother who didn't have it in her to be firm with her sons, especially an angry adolescent who resented their reclusive existence. An existence forced on him by his lynx brother.

Jonah sighed and tried to push the old memories away. He wished he could cherry-pick them, and only bring out the good ones. But pain and loss and guilt always came with them.

He reached for his notes that he'd started before Enigma arrived in to his life and tried to figure out where he'd left off in the solution. It wasn't like Jonah was solving anything important. He wasn't well enough educated for that. But the learning and the puzzling soothed him when, sometimes, nothing else could. And so he continued and pretended that one day in the far future, he would study at a university, get a degree. God knows his mother had always raved about his IQ way back when, for all the good it ever did him, or her.

Right before dusk, Jonah heard a howl, rather like the one he'd heard the day of the snowstorm before Enigma/Trey had trotted up to say hello.

He felt awkward again as he waited, but that feeling didn't last long once Trey-the-wolf appeared in the flesh, intent on getting inside, getting warm and getting something to eat. Jonah obliged him.

Then his guest lay down by the fire and fell into a deep sleep.

Not so difficult having a wolf visiting, really, thought Jonah as he returned to solving equations, feeling a strange kind of happiness at this silent companion who slept while he worked on his math. Later though, as the fire died down and Jonah drifted off, he wondered who would greet him in the morning, the wolf or the man.

Oddly enough Trey remained wolf the next day, lying near the fire and basically doing nothing. Jonah was tempted to ask him why, but didn't. Talking to a sentient wolf felt awkward.

Maybe Trey-the-human didn't like sleeping on the rug on the floor, a rather hard and cold bed. In a fit of grief, Jonah had burned Craig's cot three years ago, but it wouldn't be difficult to make another one. It was certainly the hospitable thing to do. And Jonah had come to terms with the idea that he wanted the visitor to stay for more than a couple of days. So, late in the morning, he pushed away from the fire.

He forced himself to speak, though only one word came out. "Okay."

Trey raised his large, handsome head to look at him, and

for a moment Jonah was trapped by that intense blue gaze and forgot what he was going to say.

"Um. I'm going to get some wood." Unwilling to explain he was looking for materials to make a cot, he walked off into the cave and eyed the pile of wood. What had been slated for firewood could be converted to something else. It hadn't all been chopped into smaller pieces, so he could construct a makeshift bed.

He was a rough woodworker, but Jonah knew how to make joints. He didn't say anything, just spent the day with axe and saw and a few nails to ensure the thing stayed together. Canvas, he still had from his brother's cot. He'd been careful to keep that in case it came in useful. Wood was in plentiful supply out here but not much else was.

It felt a bit odd using the canvas again, but right. Craig had hated being Jonah's brother at times, but he'd loved Jonah and would have liked Jonah to have some company after three long years. He thought. Jonah let out a sigh that caused Trey's regard to come to rest on him, his wolf's brow furrowed with question, and all Jonah said was "Almost done."

After he completed tacking the canvas to the frame, he sat back on his haunches and gazed with some satisfaction. It had been fun to have such a task to do after so many formless days in the winter. He glanced over to where Trey had lain to see his reaction. But he was gone.

Jonah had been so caught up in the work that he hadn't noticed Trey leave, and the wolf could move silently. Pushing up from his crouch, Jonah felt disappointment. For once, after finishing a project, he could announce it to someone who would understand. Not that it was the best cot ever made. Maybe Trey was unimpressed by his roughshod work. At that thought, Jonah felt his face heat up.

He bent down to clean up the mess he'd made and when he

was done, Trey strode into the room, catching Jonah unawares. He gaped, the shock no less for it being the third time Trey had shifted from wolf to human.

He was a big man, they both were, but Trey had the edge on height, breadth and muscle, which all made Jonah uneasy. His chest felt tight with emotion, and he turned to put away the last of the tools.

"So what's this?" Trey asked.

Jonah took his time to face Trey, who at least was standing now. Presumably he thought Jonah could cope with Trey at his full height. And he could, the tightness in his chest was easing or changing or something.

Trey no longer gazed at Jonah who managed to close his mouth. Instead he examined the cot and the expression on the man's face was...admiring? He turned back to Jonah and smiled. Trey hadn't fully smiled before, only hinted at such an expression, or made a restrained effort to curve his mouth. This was different and Jonah was surprised at how it changed Trey's face, made him approachable. So though Jonah felt completely tongue-tied, he managed to say, "I made it."

He rubbed the back of his neck as he realized he'd stated the obvious.

"For me?"

"If you want," he said diffidently. There wasn't anyone else he could have made it for.

"That was thoughtful of you. Thank you." With that Trey stepped over and clapped him on the back, not hard at all, and Jonah still jerked under that brief contact. Immediately Trey withdrew his arm, stepped away.

"I-I thought it would be better than the floor." Shit, he was stuttering and he hadn't stuttered since Aaron. Something about big men, even when Jonah was one.

"It will be." Trey seemed genuinely excited by what Jonah had made, and he picked up the sleeping bag he'd used that one night. As he spread it out, he said, "I couldn't face sleeping on the rug again as human, so I was going to shift tomorrow. But after I saw what you'd done, I decided not to wait. Where'd you learn woodworking?"

"My mom."

"Yeah?"

"She taught us all, including herself, when she decided we should live, um, away from civilization."

"Makes sense."

Jonah jerked a nod. It was hard to talk period, but talking about his mother and brother was the worst. And yet he added, "She was practical, in her way. Only..."

Trey waited, cocking his head. "Only what?"

"It's more complicated than you think to hide away from the world." *Especially when you decide to have asshole boyfriends.*

"I can believe that." Trey glanced around. "You've made a nice home here though."

Jonah stared, but unless Trey was playing some kind of deep game, he meant it. This wasn't Aaron, sneering away at their poverty and the tiny size of their home. "It's small."

"Needs to be small in winter, or you'll spend your entire life keeping the place warm."

"Sometimes it closes in on me," Jonah blurted. Christ, why'd he have to say that? Could he not talk like a regular person?

Trey simply looked at him in commiseration, as if he might have lived in exactly the same way. Though Jonah didn't think that was the case. Trey seemed so worldly. "Well, maybe we can work on ways to get you a bit more comfortable with your life. I think, as it is, you're too isolated."

There was a slight question in that statement, Trey looking for feedback or something, Jonah supposed. He stared at his feet before making himself meet Trey's blue gaze. With some dismay, he realized he was going to say more about himself, when he didn't want to, but he couldn't stop voicing his fear. "Sometimes I think I might go crazy."

Then Trey did this weird thing. Well, Jonah guessed it wasn't that weird, just weird for hermit woodsmen. Trey stepped up beside him and gave a one-armed shoulder hug. At first Jonah went stiff with surprise, wondering what this meant, where it was going. But nothing happened as such, just a warm arm around him. It had been so long since anyone had touched him that the sensation flowed through his entire body and something inside unwound a little.

When Trey didn't let go right away, Jonah found himself relaxing a fraction, even leaning into the hug. It felt as if a kind of relief was flooding his veins, running through his blood, a release of tension. He didn't understand it and his thoughts swam with the headiness of his reaction.

Somehow then, Trey lowered him to the cot he'd made, but instead of leaving, they sat there shoulder to shoulder, and Jonah said the next thing that came to mind.

"I think there's something wrong with me." Was this what happened when you were deprived of people for three years? You said all the wrong things? You said what was inside you that should *stay* inside you? He gulped a breath, unable to take the words back and plowing on despite his desire to shut up. "Besides the obvious. I mean being a lynx."

"There is nothing wrong with you." Trey sounded adamant, and Jonah pulled in a long breath. Remembering to breathe would help with the swimmy-head feeling. "You've done great.

58

I'm impressed with your setup here and how you handle yourself."

Jonah snorted in embarrassment, and again Trey brought his arm around his shoulders, rubbing his far arm. "You know, when I was approaching your home that first day, I was worried you'd be feral or vicious or both."

Hanging his head, Jonah resisted the urge to turn and hug Trey. How embarrassing would that be? Clearly Trey was trying to give some emotional support, that didn't mean the man wanted to be hugged by Jonah as if he were a ten-year-old boy craving his affection. He knew his growing up had warped some of his emotional responses, but this was ridiculous.

"I'm not vicious," Jonah said in a low voice. Yes, he'd killed Aaron, but he hadn't enjoyed it.

"That's clear," Trey said calmly. "You're a very personable young man."

Personable? Jonah realized he had snorted again, and promised himself he would not do it a third time.

"How old are you, Jonah?"

"Twenty-four."

"Really?"

Jonah pulled away to look at Trey's face and try to read what he meant by that one word. Before he could decide on anything, Trey did an extraordinary thing, he took Jonah's face in his large, warm hands, examining him in a slightly clinical way. Maybe making sure that Jonah's stated age was correct? Jonah repressed the shudder he felt to have his face cradled like that. It wasn't a repulsive shudder, more a welcoming one, which was almost worse because Jonah didn't know what to do with that emotion. He could barely think with those rough hands on his sensitive skin. He simultaneously couldn't wait till Trey let him go and didn't want to be released.

Then the heat of Trey's palms on his face was gone and Trey patted his shoulders twice before he rose, leaving Jonah alone on the cot, wordless.

Almost wordless. "You thought I was younger?"

Trey gave his half-smile, which Jonah was coming to realize meant affection, not cynicism. "You seem both older and younger. Which makes sense. You've had an unusual life here. But then, a lot of shifters do."

"Did you have an unusual life?"

Trey breathed in, and Jonah immediately regretted his question. It wasn't welcome. "I had a family, not a very nice one. My father was an asshole."

"My father didn't stick around," Jonah offered.

Trey nodded. "I don't find it that easy to talk about my family, but that doesn't mean you shouldn't ask questions. Just that I won't always be comfortable answering them."

"I understand," Jonah said quickly. "I find it hard to talk sometimes, even when I want to. And other times, I say too much."

Trey grinned for some reason, and Jonah felt like the sun was shining on him. Then Trey said, seemingly out of the blue, "I'm very glad to have met you, Jonah."

Chapter Six

Jesus, he had to be careful, Trey thought as he lay on his newly made cot that night, listening to Jonah breathe the slow, deep breaths of sleep. Trey should have been tired after shifting, but he was wide awake and a little alarmed by himself.

Okay, alarmed was too strong a word, but he was concerned. Jonah was a very attractive, very lonely, incredibly naïve, reclusive lynx shifter who was starved of affection. Trey needed to keep their relationship purely platonic to avoid betraying the young man's trust.

He'd touched Jonah earlier, for a couple of reasons. The lynx was skittish and Trey thought perhaps physical contact now and then would reassure him at a basic level that Trey was not here to hurt him. A body remembered who had hurt you and who hadn't. And someone, not Trey, had hurt Jonah. Also, shifters who went feral tended to crave human touch once they returned to their human state. While Jonah was definitely not feral, he had been as alone as a feral could be.

It had been the right thing to do. Jonah had responded a little jerkily at first, but he'd calmed down and then been more at ease in Trey's company. Besides, while wolves might be the shifters who most needed touch—a need Trey had managed to ruthlessly suppress—cat shifters, when human, when it came to spending time with their loved ones, tended to overcompensate for their solitary time spent as cats.

But crap, it had only been a few days and Jonah had gotten right under his skin, in a way that tempted Trey.

That was all right. Trey knew how to control himself. But he had to be careful not to create an expectation in Jonah that Trey could not meet. Because in two weeks, Trey would be walking out of here and Jonah would be left behind. Trey wished he had somewhere to take Jonah to, someone who could befriend the young man. However Trey had created a life for himself that existed of living among people who would like to destroy shifters if they discovered them.

Trey was aware of why he stayed away from his own kind. They had killed what he loved, more than once, and in more ways than one. A lifetime ago, Trey had led death to his lover, and while Jonah was in no way his lover, he would not endanger another innocent.

Too many memories of Quinn, alive and then dead, torn apart by wolves who Trey had in turn destroyed. The revenge had not been sweet. Trey had not been able to move on.

He closed his eyes and forced his mind to close down on thought; he painted a palette of rivers and lakes and blue sky in his mind's eye, and when that was completed, he relaxed enough to fall asleep.

The next morning, Trey helped out with the breakfast routine, starting the fire, doing the dishes. Jonah was back in shy, noncommunicative mode, with occasional hopeful glances at Trey. An improvement, really. It signaled he wanted Trey's company.

Trey wasn't used to being the one who made the conversational volleys and tended to avoid being put in any such situation, but *this* situation with Jonah was different in many, many ways.

Standing up, Trey stretched. "I slept well last night. Thanks for that."

Jonah ducked his head. It appeared that with those eight words Trey was embarrassing him with excessive praise. "It's fine," he mumbled. In anyone else this reaction would have been put-on, fake, but with Jonah it was alarmingly endearing.

Trey cleared his throat. "What's your project today?"

Those lynx eyes widened. "Project?"

"You usually have a project, at least that's how it has seemed to me, be it making me a cot or feeding the deer."

Jonah peered at him for a moment, as if trying to read Trey's real meaning. "Well, I haven't thought of one. Is there something you want to do?"

Trey wanted to understand everything about Jonah's life so he could figure out a way to help him. He gestured to the books. "I'm curious about your library, where you got the books from, what you use them for now."

Jonah shook his head, dismissing the books and everything about them. So Trey walked over and studied the titles. Nonfiction mostly, and a lot of technical stuff. He pulled out a few books and flipped through them to see they were math texts with equations and some history of math.

"I think you like math, Jonah."

He shrugged. "So?"

Odd response. "So, that's good."

Jonah grimaced. "Why's it *good*?"

"It's easier to be a sane shifter if you're interested in studying, keeps your human side going." A memory of his first night here, when Jonah had called him Enigma, came back to him. "You were going to tell me about the Enigma machine."

The expression on Jonah's face clearly conveyed that he

believed he was being humored, if not patronized. Obviously some asshole had belittled Jonah in the past.

"What did your mother think of you being interested in math?"

Jonah blinked at the change in subject, or maybe at the mention of his mother. "She was proud of me," he said warily.

"Good."

Jonah frowned, perhaps at that word *good* again.

"And your brother, Craig, what did he think?"

"He didn't care." Jonah shifted, almost scowling. "What are you getting at?"

"I'm wondering why you're defensive about math, that's all." He flipped through another book, mostly equations. He thought he'd be able to wait Jonah out on this as he continued to browse.

Five minutes later, the lynx proved him right by stepping up beside him. "I like algebra best. I study it, but it's hard to get the right education when I have no access to more books. Mom got these for me at a library sale years ago, before we moved up here. So my knowledge is patchy at best."

"You'd like to study at university."

Hope flared briefly on his rawboned face. "Do you think I could somehow?"

"Not immediately." Trey shut the book as Jonah's face fell. "But I'm going to work on it. There are correspondence courses, things like that."

Jonah bit his lip. "I have no money for it. The money I have I need for my yearly supplies. And I have no ID, either. My mother didn't register my birth certificate and social insurance number. She wanted to keep me off-record for my safety."

"I can see why she'd be careful. But like I said, I'll work on it. I can't make any promises though."

"I understand," Jonah said in that quick way of his, like he was trying not to expect too much.

"At least I'll get you some more books."

Jonah gazed at him, somewhere between amazed and admiring, and Trey had this terrible desire to reach an arm around the young man's neck and pull him close.

No.

"Thank you." Jonah's voice trembled with emotion and they stared at each other for longer than they should before Trey snapped his gaze away and took out another book, asked which type of math it was about.

Jonah was eager to talk, the dam of silence that had made up his last three years was gone with Trey there to listen and the young man had a lot to say. He opened up, explaining his entire library, both fact and fiction, and Trey paid close attention throughout the day to all Jonah wanted to tell him with that young, quite beautiful voice of his. It was clear that one of the reasons the lynx was so sane, despite his solitude, was because he was very engaged in intellectual human pursuits. It was going to be important to foster that.

That evening, Jonah's throat was sore from speaking so much. Yes, he'd told Trey about the Enigma machine, as well as what history of math he knew, as well as the Turing machine, as well as... Jonah felt a little embarrassed, even if Trey had spent the entire time looking completely interested. Maybe Trey was pretending to be interested, but nothing in his face or demeanor revealed anything but, well, fascination for what Jonah had to say. Which was pretty heady stuff after years alone. Before that his brother had displayed little interest in Jonah's studies.

However, Trey hadn't put his arm around Jonah again.

He shouldn't think about Trey's arms. Trey had only hugged him yesterday because Jonah had become too emotional. Which he didn't plan on doing again. Jonah didn't want to lose Trey's good opinion of him by showing weakness.

As they headed to bed, Trey announced rather abruptly, "In two days it's the full moon."

For a moment Jonah stared down uncomprehendingly as Trey settled himself onto the cot. Then he recalled the werewolf mythology. "The moon makes a difference?"

"Yup. We run at nights during the week of the full moon. It's unwise for a wolf to fight the strong pull of moonlight." In the dim firelight, Trey turned on his side and faced Jonah's cot. "Given how cold it is, I'm not going to shift back to human during the day, it'll cost me too much energy. So...do you want me around here, or should I take off for a week?"

"Here," Jonah said in a low voice, trying not to admit how much it meant to him for Trey to stay. The idea of Trey taking off was abhorrent, as if someone was snatching away a gift, a much-needed gift.

"Good. I'd rather be here anyway."

The next two days passed in a blur while Jonah hugged that knowledge to himself. Jonah was always talking about himself. He tried to ask things about Trey but it was hard, because the man didn't want his questions. He never looked angry, let alone mildly annoyed, but it was clear from the change in his body stance that Jonah's questions weren't welcome.

But where was Trey from, where did he work, and what had happened to his family, including the unstable brother? Jonah had no answers to these questions. And wouldn't for at least a week because now Trey was all wolf all the time.

Yet Jonah kept on talking when Trey-the-wolf returned for his daily sleep. His words kept flowing, until Jonah felt like he'd revealed everything there had ever been to reveal about himself to Trey as human and as wolf.

The one thing he did not, *could not*, reveal was the fact that he was attracted to Trey. Jonah swallowed at the thought, trying not to panic. It didn't matter right now, when Trey was wolf. Jonah could ignore it then, his attraction being all a memory. But when Trey-the-human returned, he was going to have to be careful not to let Trey realize Jonah's thoughts were more than friendly.

The truth was, Jonah didn't know how this had happened—or even *when*. Trey had loped off into the moonlit night and Jonah hadn't even been self-aware enough to realize he was developing a crush on the man. Or maybe Jonah had been keeping his head buried deep in the sand, stupidly longing for another hug from Trey without recognizing what that signaled. But for God's sake, when he'd first met Trey, as human, he'd almost thrown up. He'd wanted Trey to stay away from him.

The turnaround was giving him whiplash, even if he understood at an intellectual level that he'd been deprived of human companionship. Somehow, once Trey had turned wolf and Jonah had relaxed his guard, he'd lurched in the opposite direction from fear of Trey to, let's face it, *infatuation*. He couldn't stop thinking about Trey and about those few times Trey had touched him. It was clear Trey had only done so to reassure Jonah in one way or the other. Well, except that time Trey took Jonah's face in his hands to examine him. Why had he done that? And had he found Jonah wanting?

Fuck. Jonah shook his head. It would have been easy to regard Trey as a visitor, as a friend. But no, Jonah had to make it difficult for himself, had to think about Trey in other ways,

ways unwelcome to Trey. That was the key point to remember.

Jonah pulled in a long, calming breath. He needed to stop thinking along these lines. Otherwise, things were going to get awkward and unpleasant quickly. Jonah required a strength of mind he feared he didn't have. He worried about getting hard by accident and Trey being repulsed.

And so, as the days wore on and Trey's human return became imminent, Jonah became more and more tense.

Enough so that one afternoon, Trey came up and carefully licked one of Jonah's hands, rather like the first evening when he'd done it. Jonah wanted to kneel beside him and wrap his arms around the wolf, but he couldn't reveal that much of himself. What was so wrong with him that even the wolf knew he was stressed?

Then he hit on a solution to his problem and didn't know why he hadn't considered it earlier. Perhaps because Trey was around and being lynx was a solitary affair. But Jonah hadn't been cat for many days. If he shifted, some of this awful tension might dissipate, and he wouldn't feel so goddamn strange about himself.

He woke before Trey the next day. Trey was exhausted, having been out running half the night. He sure liked the moonlight. So did Jonah at times, and today and tonight he would stay lynx with Trey's wolf and run with him, if Trey allowed it.

It was odd to think of shifting with Trey in his home. Jonah felt vulnerable, and he took himself into the back room despite the fact he preferred shifting on his cot.

There he stripped, allowed the cold to seep into his skin, into his bones, and when he began to shiver, his lynx came to the surface, turning on the heat that presaged the darkness of the shift. He lay on the floor and Jonah's mind went blank. Time stopped.

He woke disoriented. As usual, he woke on his side, ribs rising and falling from the effort of shifting into lynx form. But this morning things were strange, new, when nothing had been strange and new for a long time. The smell of wolf alarmed him, given that he was stuck in the back of his own house. Generally he climbed trees to avoid these creatures; generally they didn't come close to him, because he was a large lynx or perhaps because they knew he was more than a lynx.

He found himself snarling as he rose, then heard movement, the sound of feet approaching.

Familiar that sound, and memories of Trey swam to the forefront of his brain. There he stood, the large dark wolf with vibrant blue eyes. His ears pointed forward while his tail moved in a friendly fashion, so Jonah stopped snarling, although his ears still lay flat on his head. With that Trey gave a woof and trotted out of the room. Jonah followed to find him waiting at the door, the expression on his face saying, *Ready?*

Trey's paw pressed down on the door's handle, made long ago to ensure it was easy for Jonah's lynx to leave and enter the house, and he opened the door. The wolf went through, waited while Jonah shut the door, and Trey was careful not to crowd the lynx, as if sensing that Jonah felt skittish.

That day and half the night, they spent outside. They covered a fair distance, more than Jonah's usual as Trey had better stamina. Staring at the moon as a lynx with a wolf for company was something wholly new, and Jonah could barely believe he had this companion who knew both halves of him. When Trey threw back his head to howl in the moonlight, Jonah joined in, yowling. For some reason Trey found this amusing and he shouldered the lynx.

His chest rumbling in a purr, Jonah pushed back, enough that Trey tackled him, and they rolled in the deep snow, tumbling down the not-very-steep hill until Jonah had to give up the fight. As in human form, Trey was the stronger. In apology, perhaps for having gotten carried away, Trey licked Jonah's ear and Jonah's chest rumbled again.

The tension in Jonah had eased and he didn't question it, didn't try to remember why he'd felt so restless the day before. His human would know, but he slotted that away for later, when all those human thoughts returned. For now, he enjoyed what was—company and play and a clear, clean night of moonlight and stars.

Trey took off, and Jonah chased him, though he wasn't allowed to catch him. The wolf was keen to show he was the stronger, and yet Jonah wasn't bothered because he wasn't aggressive, and sometimes he was affectionate. His lynx had rarely received affection in his life. Only his human.

When they returned home, late, they flopped down in the cold room on the rug, and finally Trey touched him again, as they huddled together for warmth.

It seemed rather amazing, and Jonah purred with happiness until he fell asleep.

Chapter Seven

Jonah woke flat-out exhausted, became aware enough to push himself up from the rug, only to find Trey-the-man had lit a fire and was eating breakfast.

"Hey, you're awake." Trey's mouth kicked up, that half-smile of his. "Go change." He jerked his head towards the back room.

Jonah rose slowly and tentatively, arching his back, extending his claws. For some reason he liked appearing big and strong in front of Trey, not to intimidate but for show. He settled on his rump, not ready to shift quite yet. They hadn't been together this way before, him as cat, Trey as human.

Trey grinned. "Very impressive. You're a beautiful lynx, I can say that."

Jonah sat stock-still for a moment, not sure what to make of such a statement. No one had ever said it before. His lynx was a burden his mother and brother had been forced to bear, and had often tried to avoid. When he was younger, Aaron had kicked him a couple times until he'd learned to stay out of sight.

Watching him carefully now, Trey said, "Come here then."

The idea of going right up to Trey appealed although the lynx in him felt wary, nervous. Trey simply waited him out. Jonah rose again and walked over to Trey who crouched by the fire, heating water for coffee, though all of Jonah's coffee was years old and stale. Trey apparently craved caffeine after he'd shifted. One of the few personal details he'd offered.

There should have been resentment about how one-sided their conversations had been, but Jonah couldn't find it in him. Mostly he was grateful to have company, to have someone who was interested in him. He brushed his chin against Trey's shoulder and, when that contact wasn't rebuffed, laid his head there. He couldn't help himself, he purred. Contact with Trey made him purr, he realized. Rarely had his chest rumbled to life like this.

Trey laughed, but not at him, it was a full-body laugh and he shifted his feet so that suddenly his arm was slung around Jonah's narrow shoulders, and Trey buried his face into Jonah's neck. Jonah continued to purr, he couldn't stop while Trey ran fingers through his fur.

"Beautiful and silky," Trey declared and they sat like that for a while, Jonah soaking up this attention of Trey's, his entire body relaxing in Trey's hold as his fingers ran over Jonah's body, over fur and muscle and bone. It felt beautiful. *He* felt beautiful, just as Trey had described him.

Finally Trey withdrew, leaving one palm on Jonah's back as he said, "Come on now, Jonah, go shift for me so we can talk. Though I'm glad we had the chance to run together."

The human contact, the fingers, Trey's breath against him—they all brought his longing to be human to the fore and he didn't want to wait any longer. With one long lick to Trey's neck, which Trey willingly accepted, Jonah stalked to the back room and flopped onto the floor. With the least struggle he'd ever had, his skin and bones went fluid and his mind went black before he shifted to human.

He woke dazed. The room was warm, as if a fire was on and someone was with him. That hadn't happened for ages, and it took a few seconds for his brain to catch up, for him to recognize that at long last, he had a visitor. The visitor was Trey, a large man with the bluest eyes and the greatest interest in Jonah.

He was kind, Jonah had to remind himself. Aaron had been fascinated by Jonah, but in a sick way, a violent way. Two years into her relationship his mother had recognized what a mistake Aaron had been, but by then it was too late and Aaron had used the power of his knowledge of Jonah's lynx over them. He'd stolen his mother's money. He'd beaten her, he'd beaten Jonah.

Jonah pushed up to sitting and shook himself. Aaron wasn't here, would never be here or anywhere else again. It was only Trey, also a shifter, who had no interest in using any power over Jonah—that he could tell. Trey seemed to actually like Jonah, and the idea he had a friend was almost overwhelming.

He felt his dick harden and his heart rate kicked up. Shit. Not *this*, not when Trey had been so kind to him. Jonah grabbed clothing and yanked it on, covering himself, trying to get himself under control. His lynx had completely forgotten this phenomenon. But every time he shifted to human, Jonah became aroused. Too much blood circulating around, he'd decided in way of explanation, but he knew that was no real cause.

He was used to taking care of himself, and in the early days when his family was around and this had started, he'd taken to shifting outside, to his mother's dismay.

But he stupidly hadn't shifted outside today and this place was too small to be masturbating unobtrusively in the back room.

Fuck. He was so furious with himself he began to shake. Jonah tried to think of other things besides Trey who would be put out, if not downright repulsed, by his obvious attraction.

Maybe Jonah would be attracted to women if he ever met any, but his wet dreams had men, not women in them, so he was rather doubtful on that count.

Trey was going to wonder, soon, what the fuck Jonah was doing back here and that realization, instead of dousing his erection, had Jonah increasingly panicked. Shouldn't panic tamp down this reaction?

It didn't. The tension was rising, all sorts of tension tied up with fear, embarrassment and this attraction he couldn't keep to himself, and Jonah could barely think. He pulled in long, deep breaths to try to calm himself, and dammit Trey must have guessed something was wrong, because he called out, "Jonah? You okay?"

Get it together. *Now.*

"Yes," he managed and bent over, feeling like he was running a race and had to stop and take a breather. To his utter dismay, he heard Trey move, heard footsteps approaching the back room, and he didn't know how to face the man like this.

God help him, he should have stayed lynx.

Trey frowned to see Jonah bent over, hands on knees, as if winded. He also smelt the tang of mixed arousal and fear in the air—Jonah's. It was a common phenomenon. When shifters turned human, they were generally hot to have sex. It had been, during another lifetime, decades ago, something Trey looked forward to. Since then he'd worked to destroy his sexual drive, taking pride in his control of all things.

It was becoming quite clear to him he'd failed. Nothing about his sexual drive felt destroyed right now.

Didn't matter. This situation was going to take a different kind of control, and some tact. He didn't want Jonah breaking down over this attraction that had grown between them, and he'd be doing Jonah no favors in continuing to pretend it didn't exist. Not when it caused these fine tremors to run through his body.

He refused to leave Jonah hanging like this, despite a dark, black part of Trey that wanted to turn around and walk away.

He couldn't.

Trey stepped forward and placed a hand on Jonah's broad back, let his palm rest on the spine that was a little bonier than it should be. Jonah needed to eat more. "Breathe."

"I am," Jonah gritted out and pulled in another noisy lungful. After an exhale, he declared, "I want some fresh air."

He barreled by Trey, out of the back room, through the main area and escaped through the front door.

Without his winter gear. Trey hoped Jonah wasn't stupid about this. A lynx who'd just shifted was a bit of a heat sink and Jonah's metabolism would be running high, so he had more time before he froze than a human. But if he wasn't back inside within ten minutes, Trey was going after him.

So he waited, watching the old wind-up, a not very accurate clock Jonah kept by his bed. At eight minutes, he grabbed Jonah's winter gear and stomped out. He wanted to give the lynx some privacy, but not at the risk of him freezing to death.

Thankfully he spotted Jonah right away, his back to him, staring out, hands on hips, still breathing hard, but less aroused, less panicked.

"Get inside," said Trey. When Jonah didn't move, Trey clamped on to his arm and pulled him back into the cave and through the door. Clearly they needed to talk. Though Trey wasn't looking forward to this at all. Especially given how he was reacting to Jonah's arousal himself. Christ. So much for control.

Inside, Jonah jerked free of Trey's grip and glared. His teeth chattered as he said, "Do you mind? I wanted a moment—"

"—to freeze your skin off?"

"I can always fucking shift if I want to, as you know."

"That's a stupid idea."

Jonah started looking pissed off, which was good, because the fear was now completely absent. Trey still wasn't sure what that fear was about. Trey pulled off the jacket he was wearing and wrapped it around Jonah, then pushed him in front of the fire.

"You need to eat," he said more softly. "You know it's a bad idea to shift when you're low on reserves and you're already skinny."

Fortunately Jonah was hungry and thirsty enough to do as Trey wished, if a little sullenly. Once he was done, he announced he wanted to go for a walk and without looking at Trey he donned his winter apparel and exited the cave.

Trey paced around the small house and sighed. He was going to have to talk to Jonah about their attraction or spend this last week with Jonah out in the snow. Maybe the latter was better, keeping an emotional distance from the young man, because God knows when Trey would get back here and Jonah deserved to have a real friend he could count on. Not some faux friend like Trey. His chest tightened, thinking of returning to his job and all that entailed.

On the other hand, he was trying to help the lynx lead a healthier life, and that probably involved some discussion of normal shifter urges and reactions. Clearly Jonah had no clue what was normal or not, had no context, being on his own like this. Jonah had been trying to hide his reaction to Trey, and continued to do so.

He was damned tempted to go after Jonah, force him back here and give him a lecture, as uncomfortable as that would be. But no—better to let Jonah calm down, let Jonah come banging into the house well past dark no worse for wear, if a little cold and hungry.

So Trey rummaged through supplies to make a supper of split-pea soup. He'd wanted bread, but found only flour, no yeast.

When the evening wind blew Jonah back inside, he saw what Trey had done for dinner and promptly seized upon the opportunity to explain about flatbreads and pans and fires. Small talk was welcomed by them both, and they got to work making yeast-free dough. Together they baked fire-cooked flatbreads and ate them with the soup. By the time the fire died down, Jonah was looking completely drained, as if he'd been through a very rough experience. He was listing to the right.

Tomorrow, Trey decided, they needed to talk, about being a shifter, about surviving alone, and maybe learning how to mix a bit with humans. He had less than a week now so there was no more putting it off. And there was no one else to do it for him. Trey did not intend to introduce wolves to Jonah's Canadian Shield sanctuary and while Trey wanted to return, he didn't know when he would be able to.

"All right," said Trey the next day in a way that made Jonah feel doomed.

Or maybe the words seemed portentous because Jonah had spent a hellish night lying awake, too wound up to sleep and worried that if he did, he'd have a wet dream with Trey in the same room. Gawd, he and his body's urges were making himself sick.

"You're looking a little peaked," Trey observed.

"I'm fine." He could barely force his breakfast down, and he was going to have to get out of here, away from Trey again. Jonah had never seen such a dubious expression on Trey's face. He tried harder to pass off his bizarre behavior. "I'm tired, that's all. Didn't sleep all that well."

"Any reason why not?"

"No." He hunched at the tone of that *no*, which sounded surly, like he was twelve years old. But God, he wasn't prepared to explain why. He had no ability to handle this gracefully.

"I think we need to have a talk."

Jonah's head shot up, and he stared at Trey, heart beginning to pound hard, worried that somehow Trey could read his mind.

"Because," Trey continued, "I'll be gone in a week, and you'll still be here. On your own."

Jonah had been studiously ignoring anything to do with the fact Trey might be departing. He didn't see what he could do about it and he didn't want to think about it. But he said, "Okay." It came out hoarser than he would have liked.

"So, I thought we should talk about strategies that could make you a little more comfortable with your life."

Jonah nodded. What the fuck was he supposed to say? There was silence, Jonah stared at his fists. Maybe it would be better when Trey was gone. At least he'd get away from this stupid tension gripping him.

"All right." Jonah pulled in a breath and met Trey's too-sharp gaze. "But I don't see what I can say about you leaving."

"This isn't about my leaving, it's about you." Trey pulled up the bench so he faced Jonah sitting on the cot, their knees close but not touching. "First off, I'd like to come back here."

"When?" Jonah said too quickly.

But Trey didn't smile at his eagerness or his, let's face it, desperation. In fact he looked more serious. "That's the problem. I don't know when. It could be months, it could be more than a year. Longer, if I'm unlucky."

When Jonah didn't respond—his heart was sinking over that amount of time, even if a part of him was gratified that Trey *wanted* to come back—Trey reached over, wrapped a hand around Jonah's knee and gave it a shake, as if he was encouraging Jonah. He felt the warmth of Trey's palm through his long johns. He had kept on a long flannel shirt to hide any unwanted reaction to Trey, which was, God help him, starting again.

"Jonah, I'd like you to actually tell me a little about what's going on inside your head."

"Well, Trey," began Jonah, irritated by the tone Trey was taking and irritated by himself for responding so sexually to what was a friendly gesture. "I'm thinking a year is a fucking long time. Is that what you want to hear?"

"Sure."

"Sure?"

"It's great to hear anything when you're trying to get a conversation going." Trey dipped his head slightly so Jonah had to meet his gaze. He didn't want to meet that gaze which saw too much, but he couldn't resist. Trey continued, "Of course it's a long time. Too long. I'm concerned about it. If I don't get back before the summer, you need to go down to the town where you buy supplies and mingle a little more."

"Mingle," Jonah repeated in disbelief.

"It's not healthy for you to stay alone up here all the time. You've done great for three years, but you can't keep pushing it."

"*Mingle*?" The anger was building and he set his jaw when he looked at Trey. "That's unsafe. I need to get in and I need to get out."

"That's your mother talking and I understand why—"

"You understand nothing," Jonah seethed. "You come in here, live with me for a few days, and before you take off you think you can tell me what I need to do to stay *healthy*?"

Trey looked annoyed, which normally would have upset Jonah, but not once he'd lost his temper. "Grow up and learn to listen to someone who has something useful to tell you."

That's it. Jonah stood, partly to get away from Trey who was too close and too warm and too intent. "You're a tourist, passing by and impressed by my woodsman-style life, and then you're gone. I don't need your advice. And I'd like to end this less-than-helpful conversation."

Trey stood too, stepped towards him, when Jonah wanted more of his own space. But he would not back up, give way. Trey, however, had gone all earnest again, not intimidating, and that made it worse because some of Jonah's anger faded and he was left with an awful yearning that made it hard to breathe.

"I am not a tourist. Like you, I'm a shapeshifter and I've done my share of living in the wild. And I will tell you that shapeshifters don't do well if they remain isolated."

"You're a *wolf*. A pack animal. I'm not. It's hard to be around you at times."

Instead of being shocked by this information, or offended, Trey's expression gentled, as if he understood that Jonah was attracted to him, which, Jesus, maybe he did. Jonah's face flushed deep red and he found he needed to get out of here, forget about standing his ground with Trey, forget about not giving way. As Jonah attempted to pass by, a hand wrapped around his upper arm and he couldn't reach the door. He tried to shake off Trey's grip.

Trey held on. "Uh-uh. You're not going out there to freeze your ass off again. You did that yesterday, remember?"

Through clenched teeth, Jonah said, "Let me go. I need some fresh air."

"For God's sakes, fresh air is about the last thing you need. I've never met someone who had so much fresh air in their life."

"Let. Me. Go." Jonah was ready to snarl.

Trey slowly released his hold, and with some dignity, Jonah stepped towards the door, careful not to act like he was bolting. He still needed to get outside. But when he reached for the handle, Trey's hand slammed down on the door, keeping it closed.

"Not today, Jonah," he said softly, and there was something beguiling about the voice, a little huskier than normal though maybe Jonah's imagination was making that up. If Trey only knew what was going on in his mind, he would be pushing Jonah out the door not holding the door shut.

Jonah stared at the hand, large and broad, powerful. Like Trey himself. He wanted to stay here, to be honest, to spend as much time as possible with Trey before he vanished, but it wasn't possible with these feelings of longing, of desire. Bowing his head, he waited it out, though what exactly he was waiting for, he didn't know. He felt like a condemned man.

"Jonah," Trey murmured.

A shiver raced through Jonah and he couldn't speak.

"Trust me a little, okay?" With that Trey ran a palm down Jonah's spine, once, twice.

It was intoxicating, that caress, and though Trey did it to reassure him, not to arouse him, Jonah's body didn't understand that. Jonah's body refused to flee, it shuddered under Trey's touch, and Trey felt it all and didn't stop. So despite all of Jonah's fears, he leaned towards Trey. When Trey didn't back away, when Trey stood strong as if ready to take Jonah's weight, he nestled in Trey's arm, asking for a hug that was easily given, and Jonah buried his face into the crook between Trey's shoulder and neck.

An awful relief flowed through him, like he'd been starving and hadn't realized it. The knowledge that Trey would have to push him away, and soon, didn't stop Jonah from lifting an arm and hugging Trey back. Still he was careful to keep his body angled away so Trey wouldn't feel his erection.

"All right" was all Trey said, in that reassuring way of his, and even if he seemed resigned, he sounded...affectionate. That was a good sign, right? Maybe Jonah wouldn't wreck everything that lay between them. They stood there for the longest time, Trey endlessly patient, until Jonah's breathing came under control. All the while Trey repeated his assurance that it was all right, that Jonah was fine.

Eventually, because it wasn't in Jonah to end this, Trey set him slightly apart, and Jonah could feel his gaze on him while he stared at the door he'd tried to escape through.

Trey cleared his throat, the noise more amused than embarrassed. "This wasn't what I planned, for all kinds of reasons, and I'm willing to explain some of them, but...you've convinced me we need to take care of you."

Despite being puzzled by Trey's words and by the suggestive tone of his voice, Jonah couldn't look up and see what was on Trey's face. Not quite yet.

Then ever so lightly, Trey passed a hand over Jonah's rock-hard but flannel-covered erection. He would have jumped twenty meters, except Trey's arm around his shoulders held him steadily in place so he jerked under Trey's hold. When he lifted his eyelashes to look at Trey, there wasn't censure or anger on the wolf's face. Just a strange openness Jonah had never seen before.

Then Trey smiled.

Chapter Eight

Jonah gaped while his heart started jackhammering again.

Trey shook his head. "What am I going to do with you?"

At the moment, Jonah had no clue, bewildered that Trey was okay with his erection. What were the odds that Trey liked men too?

"Okay, let's get some things out in the open."

It wasn't even in Jonah to nod, but he didn't have to as Trey ran a hand down his arm, linked their hands together and pulled him over to the recently made cot. Trey pushed Jonah down to sit then straddled the cot so he surrounded Jonah. He felt a bit like a puppet while Trey lifted Jonah's knees across Trey's muscular thigh. Trey's bent leg rested against Jonah's back.

"You've been deprived of human contact, human company. You know that." Instead of demanding a response, Trey nuzzled Jonah's neck, his beard rasping skin, his tongue lapping lightly as if for a taste. Jonah shivered in Trey's arms.

Trey took Jonah's chin in his hand and forced him to look directly at him. "Have you been with anyone, Jonah?"

Jonah blinked, mesmerized by how large Trey's pupils were. It made the blue irises deepen in color.

"Sexually, I mean," Trey clarified. "You're going to have to give me some answers here, because I have this thing about consent and I'll need it from you before anything happens between us."

Jonah swallowed, tried to pull together his ragged self-control and understand what Trey was asking of him. His dick was so hard, he was almost crying from want of relief, and he thought if Trey nuzzled him again, he might come then and there.

What Trey would make of that, he didn't know and he couldn't think far enough ahead to care.

"All right," Trey said and held him until Jonah found he could talk into Trey's shoulder.

"No one. There's never been...opportunity."

"That's what I thought," Trey murmured. "Okay, you have to tell me what you want now."

Jonah set his teeth and spoke. "I jerk off after I shift back to human. Otherwise, I can't think clearly."

"You want to go ahead now?"

He pulled back to see if Trey was laughing at his expense but he was serious.

"Or I can give you a helping hand..."

Jonah thought if his flaming-red face became any hotter he was going to self-combust. Trey must have seen something because his eyelids went to half-mast and he placed a palm on Jonah's hot cheek.

Next thing he knew Trey's mouth connected with Jonah's and Trey's tongue swept inside, meeting Jonah's tongue, tangling them together. Trey's palms cradled Jonah's face as Trey continued this invasion that felt simultaneously rough and gentle, forceful and coaxing.

Someone was moaning and Jonah realized it was him. Sensation ripped through him, stronger than ever before. His back arched, and Trey kissed deeper, exploring the cavern of Jonah's mouth while Jonah tried to keep up. He could barely think. His balls tightened and he held on to Trey's shoulders as a primitive noise rose from his chest. White fire flushed through his blood. He couldn't breathe and Trey breathed for him as his dick released its iron hold on what was left of his self-control. His entire body stiffened during his release, all the while Trey held him and kissed him. It was such a relief to have let go when someone was there holding him.

Jonah sagged in Trey's embrace and Trey tamped down the kiss and withdrew. He leaned his forehead against Jonah's, maybe because he was gripping so hard on Trey's shoulders, as if that was the only thing still holding him together. "Oh my God," he breathed.

"I guess you didn't need a helping hand," Trey said wryly.

Jonah felt dimly aware he should be unhappy he'd ejaculated like this, dampening his clothes, but the release and the exhaustion pulled at him while Trey's presence reassured him, and he didn't give in to the embarrassment. "I can't believe this," he managed. "I—" He frowned, tried to form words more coherently. "Are you *attracted* to me?" he blurted, dumbfounded.

At the question, Trey grinned. "Yup."

With that, Trey tugged off Jonah's long underwear, mopping him up a bit while Jonah found himself gaping again. With a matter-of-fact pat on Jonah's still semi-hard cock, Trey said, "Very pretty."

Jonah felt like he'd entered some alternate reality and he didn't know any of the rules. Still, he ventured to ask, "What about you?"

Trey winked. It seemed so un-Trey-like. But somehow this encounter—could you call it sex?—had loosened up Trey too. "I'm older. We can worry about me later."

"What are the chances that you'd be attracted to me?" Jonah persisted, because he couldn't quite let it go, even if his body was demanding he sleep after the release and the tension and sleeplessness of the past few days.

"It's not that incredible." Trey was watching him now, trying to assess something.

"Do all shapeshifters like men or something?"

"No."

"Just us?"

"No." Trey crouched by the cot, ran fingers through Jonah's hair and if Jonah had been lynx, he would have purred. "But it's more likely in the shifter population than human population. Not sure why. May or may not be related to the fact there are more male than female shifters."

"Oh."

Trey lifted up the sleeping bag. "Get inside and stay warm. The fire's died down and I need to stoke it again."

Jonah obeyed, lacking any brain cells at the moment to be anything but obedient. But as Trey turned away, Jonah's arm crept out from the sleeping bag he'd crawled into. He grabbed Trey's hand. He suddenly had this terrible fear that Trey would disappear now, after what had happened. "You'll be here when I wake up?"

Trey nodded. "I promise."

Jonah didn't release Trey right away, and Trey didn't protest. Right before he fell asleep, he felt Trey kiss the back of his hand and place it down.

Kissing. He'd never thought Trey would kiss him.

What the hell had he been thinking, kissing Jonah? That wasn't how Trey had meant it to go. It was supposed to be fuck-buddy sex. Matter of fact. Physical more than emotional. Friends with benefits. Whatever other clichéd phrase he could come up with.

But then Jonah had been so absolutely wound up, so wired, panicked, and it hadn't been in Trey to leave Jonah on the hook like that, no matter the rationale for not getting too involved. There would be fallout, yes, and it would be hard to face, especially for Jonah. But it wasn't as if Jonah had been having an easy time before Trey had kissed him. Trey had felt desperate to reach through the lynx's tension and connect at some level so Jonah could find his way to release.

Well, I guess I succeeded. And if he cared to be honest with himself, he couldn't regret it. Not now.

Jonah slept most of the afternoon while Trey kept the fire going, washed a few clothes and peered at different dried goods trying to figure out what their next meals should be. Something simple. Because he had no doubt they were going to be busy over the next few days. With each other.

Trey grimaced then, feeling like a hypocrite. All his arguments about keeping a certain distance between himself and Jonah had gone up in smoke, and he feared there was a strong element of selfishness at its base, despite his rationalizing what he'd initiated today. He'd spent years alone, with few physical encounters and those with strangers. He'd taken pride in his asceticism, his self-control. And now that an opportunity for something else had arisen, he was throwing that part of himself away.

He scrubbed his face. He was almost forty. Not terribly happy or satisfied. He was going into a difficult and dangerous situation soon, undercover in an agency that would lock him up and dissect him if they knew he was a werewolf. And he'd looked forward to it, looked forward to the self-punishment. He was a whore for punishment. Quinn had told him that once, but they'd been laughing. It had been about Trey's marathons then, which he'd always been running. But it had been about more than that too.

He'd fallen hard for Quinn. This wasn't the same situation, far from it. For one thing, Quinn had been older. But if Trey was honest, he could admit he was falling for a raw-boned, untried man who was barely more than a youth, if not in age then in experience.

He'd never before found inexperience appealing or attractive, but he hadn't met Jonah before either. Trey poked the fire, this time smiling. There were no preconceptions here, no expectations. Their relationship, short as it would be, would play out without the burden of cynicism or bitterness or game playing.

Jonah stirred and Trey shifted so he could see. He hoped the panic and fear would be, if not gone, at least substantially reduced. Trey had been concerned that the fear had something to do with a bad sexual experience, some kind of abuse, but that didn't seem to be the case. He still wanted to understand it though.

Jonah's eyelids lifted and suddenly awake, he shoved up to sitting as his gaze landed on Trey. Wide eyed, a little uncertain, Jonah looked appealingly rumpled with sleep. Trey could smell his arousal and smiled.

"Good evening."

"Thanks for keeping the fire going and..." Jonah glanced at the small line where his long underwear hung to dry, as well as a couple of other items of clothing. His face flushed and Trey's cock responded. No more second-guessing. That would come later. He pushed off the bench and stalked over to the cot, then swung a leg around so he straddled the cot again and sat between Jonah's legs. He was going to have good memories of this cot, he knew it.

Jonah's eyes grew darker and greener.

"And?" Trey asked.

"What?"

But Trey didn't wait for an answer. He laid a palm against Jonah's neck and Jonah leaned into him.

"I can smell your arousal."

"Oh God." Jonah's gaze skittered to the side and he sounded aghast. "*Always?* All this time you've smelled it?"

"Well, yeah. I'll admit I was flattered."

"Flattered?" Jonah spluttered, caught somewhere between relief and embarrassment.

"Sure. Cute young guy like you..."

The expression on Jonah's face, if it could have been translated into words, was *What are you talking about?* But he didn't say that. His chest heaved once and he moved on to say, "I thought you'd be angry. Maybe repulsed. I tried so hard to control it."

It. So Jonah's working vocabulary about sex was limited, mainly by bashfulness, Trey would guess, though ignorance was probably at work here too. Had Jonah's mother had any sex-education talks with her son? There certainly weren't any handbooks to be found around here.

In any event, perhaps this was the source of Jonah's fear— that Trey would be angered by Jonah's attraction, Jonah's arousal. "It doesn't make me angry," he said softly. "It turns me on. You can probably smell mine, you know, if you learn to identify it."

Jonah glanced down at Trey's crotch.

"What do you want, Jonah?"

Jonah eyed him, licking his lips, and Trey had the sense that Jonah wanted too much and didn't know how to articulate any of it. But there were ways of gaining consent, so Trey pulled down the sleeping bag and slipped a hand over Jonah's bare hip. Jonah jolted slightly at the touch, and Trey waited until he'd gotten acclimated to that.

"I'm sorry," Jonah managed rather breathlessly, but his expression was lighter now, the fear banished.

"What are you sorry for?"

"I love everything you do, but I'm not used to any of it." The last words came out hoarsely as if they were a little hard to say.

"We have some days to work on that."

"Yeah. Yeah."

"I wish we had longer, I really do." Trey stroked that hip, not going far, enjoying the way Jonah's breathing changed, his arousal increasing, his eyes darkening. Talk about responsive. Maybe at twenty-four years of age, and a virgin, a shifter had a lot of catching up to do. Trey slid a hand down Jonah's chest, over the thin cotton material, and brought it to rest on the other hip. This time Jonah didn't jolt, but he rose, as if to meet Trey, and Trey leaned in to nuzzle Jonah's neck, lick the salt and musk that was so intoxicating.

His cock liked the smell too and strained to be released. Trey would indulge himself this round, even if it simply meant taking himself in hand. He had no idea how easily or difficult Jonah would approach such a task. His isolation and, Trey suspected, some strange ideas of sex from his unusual upbringing, had made Jonah more than a little unknowledgeable about shifters and sex.

Trey pulled back. "You're going to have to give me permission to touch you."

Jonah blinked. His voice came out hoarse and throaty and utterly appealing. "You can touch me anywhere. Everywhere."

Trey suddenly had a vision of turning Jonah over,

spreading his ass wide open and rimming. But Jonah wasn't there yet, not at all, so instead he slid his hands back and under Jonah, lifting him out of the sleeping bag.

Jonah's beautiful cock stood up, weeping for attention, and with one finger Trey lightly touched Jonah's slit, enjoying Jonah's harsh gasp as he spread the precome around the head and down his length. Trey sensed that if he used his entire hand, Jonah would go off again and Trey wasn't ready for that quite yet.

He looked at Jonah, whose eyes went unfocused when Trey caressed his balls, made tight by Jonah's need to come.

"You're almost there," Trey murmured. He pinched one ball, enough to cause a little pain and pull Jonah back from the edge. "Not quite yet."

Jonah's breathing was ragged now, his body tense, and Trey knew he wasn't going to come with him this time. Maybe next time.

"I have an idea." Trey wrapped a hand around the back of Jonah's head in order to bring his mouth in for a kiss. Trey took Jonah's mouth, full on, going deep, but keeping it brief. He nipped that bottom lip as he retreated. "Trust me?"

"*Yes.*" Jonah's entire body felt hot and needy under Trey's hands. And under his mouth. He backed up and bent over, taking Jonah's steel-like cock to the back of his throat while he anchored Jonah by his hips, keeping him down on the bed.

Good thing, as Jonah reacted by almost arching right off the cot, a harsh groan echoing as Trey retreated, swirled his tongue around the sensitive glans and again full-throated Jonah.

Jonah came at once, shaking and shivering, salty-sweet come filling Trey's mouth, deep needy noises sounding from his throat. He fell back as Trey kept licking his cock, cleaning up all the milky fluid that pulsed out. Trey enjoyed exploring, probing the slit with his tongue, lapping at the large vein running down the underside.

When Jonah was finished and Trey could hear him breathing raggedly, he still didn't stop. Instead he kissed his way down Jonah's shaft to suck one ball into his mouth. Jonah gasped as Trey applied careful pressure to one then the other ball. He licked back up Jonah's cock, felt it stiffen as he took him fully to the back of his throat again and again.

Next, he licked up to Jonah's belly button. God, it had been so long since he'd explored someone's body. It was intoxicating and his own cock was aching now. But he continued his slow perusal, kissing upwards until he took a small stiff nipple into his mouth, bit lightly to feel Jonah jerk in reaction, then soothed it with his tongue. He paid careful attention to the other nipple and smiled as Jonah was again arching under his ministrations.

He lifted his gaze to Jonah, who stared back in rapt wonder. And for the first time, Jonah reached for him, placed a hand on Trey's jaw. "You're like magic to me."

Jonah palmed Trey's neck.

"Take off my long underwear." Trey watched Jonah's face for any sign of distress at the command, but Jonah reached and pulled, helping Trey divest himself of the clothing.

Somehow they ended up sitting then, facing each other, arms around each other, legs against each other. Jonah placed a hand on Trey's chest and slowly dragged it down as Trey had earlier. There was a question on Jonah's face, so Trey nodded. With some tentativeness, Jonah wrapped a hand around Trey's dick.

They seemed mesmerized by each other as Jonah slid his hand up and down, finding a rhythm he'd probably used on himself.

It had been a long time. Trey had purposefully trained himself not to need masturbation, not wanting to need anything. Even now he kept himself silent, unable to make the kinds of noises Jonah had so easily shared earlier, unable to give himself away in that manner.

He hardened further under Jonah's ministrations but Jonah asked into Trey's silence, "Is this how you like it?"

The uncertainty there caught like a hook in Trey's chest and if he couldn't let himself make noises, he could say, "It's perfect, you're perfect," and he kissed Jonah to prevent any more questions. He also took Jonah's cock in his own hand, because the responsiveness, the hardness there, had him focused on nothing else in the world but Jonah and himself and what their bodies could give to each other.

Between the kissing and that large, warm hand urging him to give over and let his body release what needed to be released, Trey felt heat flush through him. It was a precursor, a warning—as if his body was out of practice when it came to sex. A rumble, low and restrained, *his*, surprised him. His muscles seized and then he let go, gave over to the moment, not quite blindness, but no longer alert, in control. Wet heat flowed over his hand. He became disoriented, coming and feeling his come simultaneously, until he realized that Jonah had ejaculated at the same time he had. Jonah was shivering again, whimpering a little, his breathing uneven, and Trey, silent but grateful, pulled him to his chest.

Jonah wrapped his arms around Trey and held tight. He turned his face towards Trey and licked along his collarbone. Trey couldn't help but laugh. "We need to take a break and figure out what to have for supper or we'll starve."

Instead Jonah sucked at Trey's neck, hard enough to leave a mark. "I like the taste of you." He sounded surprised.

"Yeah, well, it's not going to give you any calories no matter how much you do that." Trey pulled him away and Jonah lifted himself to mold their mouths together. While Trey meant to let Jonah kiss him, he found himself digging a hand into Jonah's hair and going all out in a deep kiss he couldn't stop himself taking over. He rose above Jonah on a tide of selfishness, asserting himself and bending Jonah back slightly. Maybe it was selfish not to let Jonah control the kiss, but Trey had reacted before he thought it through. In recompense he gently stroked Jonah's neck, feeling the soft noises of need vibrating from his voice box.

He gentled the kiss, surprised by his feeling of possessiveness, and slowly extracted himself from Jonah's embrace.

"Oh my God, I'm hard again," said Jonah, sounding at sea, and Trey barked with laughter.

"Hold on there for half an hour, okay? And then we'll see what we can do to take care of you. Again. First, I need your help in the kitchen."

The fire had died down, so they threw on some clothing and Jonah, despite the distraction of his hard-on, found some easy-to-throw-together meal. They ate lentil mush and beef jerky, quickly and efficiently. Then they went to the great-outdoors restroom. At which point Trey said, as he slapped his now-cold arms after being outside, "Time to warm up, I think."

Chapter Nine

Sometime during the next couple of days, Trey woke up lying across Jonah's chest, a sleeping bag thrown over his back. He couldn't remember the last time that had happened. He'd woken with Quinn, yes, many times, but Quinn had been quite a bit smaller than him. If Trey had lain on Quinn, he would have smothered him.

Jonah, however, was pretty solid and took Trey's weight easily, awake or asleep.

Carefully, so as not to rouse Jonah, Trey eased up, and was immediately clasped tight and held down. Trey met Jonah's gaze, bright in the barely lit cabin. The fire had died down, so little illumination filled the cabin.

"I'm crushing you," Trey pointed out.

Jonah smiled. "I like you crushing me."

"I'm surprised you can breathe, let alone sleep." But Trey let his body weigh down on Jonah again, absorbing the lynx's heat as well as the vibrations that came from Jonah's breathing and heartbeat.

"This isn't when I have trouble breathing." Jonah's lids fell for a moment, almost shy at referring to sex. Then he traced a pattern on Trey's shoulder. "Waking up with you is almost—" He paused, picking his words carefully. "I was going to say as good as, but that's not what I mean. Waking up with you is as important as the sex. I didn't know that."

Trey lifted his head and recognized, not for the first time, that they were both in deeper than he'd meant them to be, but also recognized that he'd been a fool to think he could control this. If he'd tried to, he would have simply broken what was between them and that would have harmed Jonah as much as the leave-taking that was bearing down upon them. It weighed on Trey's mind, but Jonah seemed to be ignoring it.

Trey swallowed once. "It's not always important. Sometimes it's only sex. No waking up with someone."

Jonah frowned. "I don't think I'd like that as much."

"Yeah, well."

He resumed tracing a pattern on Trey's skin. "Can I ask you a question?"

"Sure." In fact, Trey dreaded Jonah's questions, feared they'd be something he found difficult to speak about. But onc of his trade-offs for continuing to have sex with Jonah—to make love, let's admit it, even if they had so far stuck to mutual masturbation and oral sex—was that he'd be as honest with Jonah as he knew how. No deception, no brushing Jonah off. The young man deserved at least that respect from Trey, whose iron control of the last twenty years had been destroyed. Trey had been more fragile than he realized. Or more vulnerable. Or maybe it was just Jonah.

"Earth to Trey."

Trey focused. "Sorry."

"How many lovers have you had?" Jonah bit his lip and added quickly, "You don't have to answer that. I'm just curious. Probably too curious."

Not such a difficult question. It didn't demand he speak of Quinn. Trey dipped his head down to mouth Jonah's neck. The first day, that would have been enough to make Jonah come, but now, while his lover hardened, he didn't immediately seem set for take-off. Something about having sex seven times yesterday did that to a guy. Even a twenty-four-year-old insatiable guy.

"I don't mind the question." Trey explored under Jonah's arm, enjoying the strong musk that belonged only to Jonah. The body under him rippled in satisfaction. He nipped Jonah's biceps and pushed away, thinking. "But I'm not entirely sure."

"Oh."

"I had kind of a crazy youth. A bit sex-crazed, I guess." Actually that was a stupid way to describe the way his pack had encouraged their young to go at each other during the full moon. It had been unhealthy and sometimes violent. But he turned away from those thoughts, seeing that Jonah was frowning in concern. "Then later, very few. Too much and then too little, I suppose."

Jonah pulled him close, angling his mouth for a kiss, and Trey gave it to him. He didn't insist he control everything, he wanted Jonah to take the lead sometimes, but Trey had a hard time not being the driving force behind the kisses. But he never felt resistance, never felt that Jonah wanted him to stop. Jonah seemed primed to take and take and take. As well as give, for Jonah held him, warm hands roaming over Trey's back.

Trey broke off. He had some ideas. There were three days left and he figured it was time for he and Jonah to try something a little new. "Let's wash up."

He rose, disengaging their bodies which were rather stickily joined together, and Jonah blinked, surprised. "Now?"

Trey bent down and lightly bit Jonah's left pink nipple. "You'll see what a great idea this is."

The wariness of the first day was completely gone, only anticipation lit Jonah's face as he said, "Okay."

They stoked up the fire and Trey went out to get snow to melt for the baths. He liked dirty sex as much as the next guy, but not for what he wanted to happen next.

"I think we'd better eat something, so we don't have to eat later."

Jonah cocked his head at that. "How long is this going to take?"

Trey knew he was smirking, but he simply shook his head. "Don't ask."

"All right." He watched Trey carefully, curiously, completely trusting. Something turned over in Trey's chest, but he needed to keep this light, not heavy, even if the realization that he was thinking of Jonah as his mate could no longer be ignored. *That* wasn't something he could share with the lynx. Not now, when he was soon abandoning Jonah, leaving him to his isolation. Maybe later, when things could be changed between them—if a later happened.

Light, he reminded himself. After all, there was joy to be found in sex and he meant for Jonah to know that. Trey took on a teasing tone. "I know you're fast"—Jonah was not self-conscious about his hair trigger and Trey wanted him to stay that way—"but I'm not. We'll try to do something to even that out."

Clearly baffled, Jonah said, "I don't know what you're talking about."

"That's all right, sometimes it's better to show than tell."

Jonah eyed him like he was hungry and Trey was the most delicious thing he'd seen a long time. Of course Trey had been under the gaze before, had been wanted and desired. But for a long, long time only by men he'd known in passing. He'd forgotten how it felt, to receive this look of desire. It warmed his blood. It made him smile.

"Well?" demanded Jonah.

The eager impatience had Trey laughing, but he pointed to Jonah's dish. "Eat."

"I am. You're the one who's forgetting." And it was true, Trey felt very distracted, but he got himself to eat the food Jonah had thrown together though he barely tasted it. When they were done, Trey stoked the fire higher so Jonah would stay warm when he was naked and wet. Trey's cock was already stiff and Jonah noticed, reached over to slide a hand up and down.

"I can take care of that," Jonah said in a low voice.

"I know you can." Trey was rather gratified by how easily Jonah had taken to licking and sucking him. It was tempting to just go with it, but then he wouldn't have the energy for what he really wanted. Still he allowed Jonah to continue to caress him, turn him on. He wasn't going to touch Jonah's dick now, because he knew exactly when he wanted Jonah to come, and it wasn't yet. Jonah tugged up Trey's shirt to explore Trey's chest, and Trey gave over to the sensation, lines of desire running through his body.

Before it got too intense, he carefully pulled Jonah's head away from him, and Jonah looked up, clearly expecting his mouth to be ravished. Suddenly feeling fierce Trey obliged, smashed lips together and plundered. Jonah's hand dropped away from Trey's cock as he simply tried to keep up with the kiss. Trey sucked on Jonah's tongue, then dipped deeper, exploring that sweet, warm cavern, tangling again with Jonah's tongue before nipping lips, because he loved seeing Jonah's mouth swollen and well kissed, seeing Jonah's face open and wondering and ready for whatever came next.

Before Jonah could ask, Trey lifted off Jonah's shirt and pushed him down to sit on the bench as close to the fire as possible without getting scorched. Next, Trey dipped his hands into Jonah's pants and pulled off everything, to leave Jonah

100

nude on the bench.

Jonah's lips curved as he smiled up at Trey. "I see you're going into command mode."

He wasn't off the mark. Trey knew he had a few control issues and could switch from fully in control to passive. Jonah might think that was normal, though Jonah didn't react in quite the same way. Which was good. "Do you mind?" he asked softly.

Jonah shook his head and spread his legs wider in invitation. His long beautiful cock stood at attention, hard and wanting, a bead of pearly come forming on the slit.

Trey couldn't resist saying, "You won't have to wait long. I promise."

"God." Jonah shifted. "I'm getting more turned on just by sitting here while you look at me."

"As you should." Trey reached for the washcloth and soap. He started with Jonah's face.

"Jesus, I can wash my face." It wasn't quite a protest as a "what's going on?" statement and Trey answered it by kissing Jonah deeply as he trailed the washcloth over Jonah's chest. Then he backed up, rinsed and washed Jonah's limbs.

"Hold out your arms so they dry by the fire."

Jonah complied, though he trembled with the effort. "Trey," he said in warning.

"Yes?" Now Trey was washing Jonah's back and a part of him wanted to forget about this slow seduction. His cock was hard and aching, and he imagined pushing Jonah on all fours and fucking him.

Another time. He wasn't quite sure Jonah knew about anal sex, his education so strangely spotty, entirely dependent on which books his mother had managed to pick up at the few library sales she'd plundered. Trey had toyed with the idea of

101

discussing anal sex beforehand, but decided a demonstration was in order. He knew they might not actually engage in intercourse, but he thought he could convince Jonah that anal play had its rewards.

Trey tweaked Jonah's nipple and Jonah forgot what he was asking. He rinsed and sudsed the cloth again, brought it to Jonah's engorged penis.

"Jesus, that feels good. You're taking so long to touch me." Still Jonah kept his arms out but now his body was shaking.

"Arms down," Trey said softly as he cleaned Jonah's head, shaft and balls.

Jonah placed an arm on Trey's. "I think I'm getting a little embarrassed. You're not going to…"

"Patience."

"What kind of answer is that?"

"Back up and bend forward."

"Trey."

But Trey didn't answer, he just placed one hand on Jonah's cock, thumb stroking the slit how Jonah liked it. With his free arm, he bent Jonah forward. "Trust me," he murmured.

Then he dipped the cloth in and began washing Jonah's ass, the cheeks first.

"I trust you." Jonah's breathing was choppy now. "But what are you doing?"

"Cleaning you."

"But why?"

"Does it turn you on?"

No answer.

"It turns me on. You're so beautiful." Trey ran the cloth along Jonah's crack, not stopping at the hole, but running back and forth.

Panting, Jonah's face had flushed deep red. Trey paused to rinse the cloth and again ran the soft cloth up and down the crack, over and over Jonah's tender hole.

"Trey?" This time there was no warning in Jonah's voice, rather a question, thready, unsure, asking for reassurance.

"I'm here," and Trey pumped Jonah's weeping cock once but no more, not wanting him to come yet. He let go of the washcloth and picked up the soap, made his hand slick and dropped it. "Turn your head and kiss me."

Jonah twisted his neck, opened his mouth, and Trey dived in, reassuring with his tongue and lips, waiting for Jonah's breath to even out and for the kiss to distract him from what was next. Once Jonah's tongue began mating with Trey's, he ran a finger across Jonah's crack and he stiffened again, pulled back, eyes wide and dark and blurred with passion.

They stared at each other as Trey traced a soapy finger around the tight outer muscle of Jonah's anus.

"Ungh." Jonah let his head fall on Trey's shoulder.

Trey took that as a yes and pushed through, his slick finger sliding in easily.

Jonah stiffened again, lifting his head, staring at Trey who didn't move. There was no fear or distress in Jonah's open face, only question.

"Okay?" asked Trey, wrapping his palm around Jonah's cock.

"Oh my God." Jonah's chest heaved once, his entire body tightening, a signal he would come.

So Trey released Jonah's cock, not willing for it to be over yet, at least that way. He slid his finger in and out of Jonah whose gaze went unfocused, whose arms came around Trey's middle, holding on hard. Tight gasps came panting out of Jonah, and Trey had this terrible, strong desire to turn him sideways and impale him on his cock.

Slow, slow, he told himself and pulled out that finger, traced the responsive outer muscle. Then he removed his finger and sat beside Jonah, breathing hard himself.

All of a sudden Jonah pushed back and took himself in hand.

Trey moved quickly, grabbing Jonah's wrist. "No."

"I didn't come," Jonah protested.

"Neither did I," Trey pointed out.

"Jesus, Trey, I think we can figure out a way to fix that. I'm so fucking close. Are you?"

"Did you like that?"

Jonah's jaw dropped. "We're going to analyze this now? No fucking way." He shifted to straddling the bench, facing Trey.

"We better before I fuck you."

"Fuck my mouth." Jonah pulled at Trey's waistband, freeing his dick. He wrapped a strong hand around Trey. "Jesus, you're hard. Why are you punishing us both?"

Before Jonah could lower his mouth to Trey, he grabbed his lover in both hands and kissed. Jonah fought, wanting more, wanting to touch Trey or himself, and Trey found himself pushing Jonah backward, caging his arms to his sides so the only thing Jonah could do was kiss Trey back. This time Jonah wouldn't let Trey keep control of the kiss, even if he was under Trey, being crushed by his weight. Eventually Trey gave up controlling their mouths, as long as he controlled the rest of what Jonah was doing, and Jonah delved deep into Trey, a kind of fury in his kiss.

It took a while for Jonah to end it and they lay there, Trey resting his forehead against Jonah's. "I told you to be patient."

Jonah's eyes were huge, and he lifted his legs to bracket

Trey's body. "Fuck me."

"Do you know what you're saying?"

"I can put two and two together."

"Anal intercourse, have you heard of it?"

Jonah shook his head.

"It means I fuck your ass. I can make it good for you. Is that what you want?"

Jonah nodded once, breathing heavily.

"It might hurt, the stretching. You can tell me to stop at any time."

"Okay." One word, a bare murmur.

"What did you think of my finger in you?"

"*Trey.* You talk too much."

Trey grinned. "Let's go over to the cot." Then he rose, gathering the oil Jonah used for cooking. He plopped down on the cot to face Jonah, poured some oil in the palm of his hand, and slicked up his cock, watching Jonah watch him pump himself.

Slowly, Jonah sat up from the bench, his eyes now lidded, a sultry expression on his face that dispelled all of Trey's fears—this had nothing to do with violence—and he walked over to Trey.

"I talk too much, eh," said Trey as he turned Jonah around and maneuvered him so he was face down on the cot, rump in the air. He palmed the hard muscle of Jonah's ass. Beautiful. Yeah, it was nicer to face each other, but Trey felt he'd have more control this way, less likely to hurt Jonah. Facing each other would have to happen another time.

"Not really," said Jonah, voice muffled by the bedding. A little subdued. Perhaps he expected Trey to plunge in.

Trey bent down far enough to lick Jonah's sac, then suck

on his balls.

"Oh," said Jonah, almost like relief, and Trey suspected he was hoping Trey would pump his dick. Not yet, though. Trey released Jonah's sac and lapped backward, over Jonah's hole, and was rewarded by Jonah's groan. Back and forth he went, then around, teasing the opening with his tongue, convincing Jonah to loosen.

The throaty moan had begun, accompanied by, "Trey, I need to come or I'm going to die."

Trey removed his mouth from eating Jonah's ass. "Soon, I promise."

Then he placed the head of his slick cock against Jonah's soft entrance, didn't push, simply held it there. Jonah tensed a little and Trey slid a hand between Jonah's legs to wrap fingers around Jonah's shaft. "Don't worry, Jonah. You need to come."

"God, yes."

"I want you to come." He just held the too-hard cock. "Can you come like this?"

"Yes, no, maybe." Jonah was panting again.

"I love the noises you make when we're making love," Trey murmured, and Jonah keened while Trey traced his slit with his thumb. "Can you come like this?"

"Ugh."

Trey pumped once. At the same time he applied some pressure to Jonah's hole, the head of his cock sensitive against Jonah's warm, tender tissue. Trey feared he'd go off before he entered Jonah. Though God knows there were worse things to fear.

The ragged breathing encouraged Trey and he pumped again, pushed further.

"*Trey,*" Jonah shouted and his anus opened, letting Trey

slide in just as his cock released its seed into Trey's moving hand. Trey didn't stop moving up and down Jonah's now-slick-with-his-own-come cock, didn't stop caressing Jonah's shaft and head, even while he slid all the way home, his balls to Jonah's butt.

Something deep and guttural emerged from Jonah's chest, and Trey ran a palm along Jonah's spine, not moving, now that he was home. It had been so long since he'd done this, and never when it had felt so right. Quinn had only topped.

"Jonah? You need to tell me how you are."

"I don't know." He sounded winded, exhausted. Still adjusting to Trey being inside him.

"Should I pull out?"

"*No.* God, no. I just..." He slammed the cot with his fist. "Overwhelmed."

"We can stop." With supreme effort, Trey started to pull back and Jonah's muscles clenched around him.

"No." Jonah gasped as Trey pushed back in. "Jesus, so much...no stopping. Please, Trey."

"Should we stay like this then?"

"What?"

"Did you like the movement or do you like me staying still?"

Jonah's body was trembling under his now, from the effort of keeping up, keeping his legs bent. It took a bit of work, but Trey slid his legs under Jonah and lifted him so he sat impaled on Trey's lap, Trey's feet on the floor and Trey's arms wrapped around him. More intimate.

"Better?"

Jonah lolled his head back on Trey's shoulder, and he touched Jonah's cheek to turn him to face Trey. They kissed, Trey gentle now that all the fight had gone out of Jonah.

Coming did that to a person, as did someone inside you the first time. This new position made it difficult for Trey to move, but maybe it was just as well. He wasn't sure how much movement Jonah was ready for, and he wasn't sure if he'd last a minute once he started his strokes.

So he kissed and caressed and nuzzled, tweaking Jonah's nipple, running a palm down Jonah's firm, muscled abdomen. They had all the time in the world now that he was inside Jonah. After a while, Trey wasn't surprised to find Jonah had hardened again under all this stimulation.

"You're back," Trey murmured, yet again stroking Jonah, thinking about his own cock deep inside, ready to blow. He shifted, lifting Jonah slightly, a small stroke that nevertheless stimulated him, while bringing Trey closer to the edge.

Jonah whimpered.

"You were worried about coming earlier," Trey whispered as Jonah hardened further. "But now I want you to come again."

"I can hardly breathe. You're so big, so close."

Trey placed a palm on Jonah's chest. "Breathe, baby, breathe."

"I want you." Jonah's entire body trembled now, as it did sometimes when he was close.

"You have me." He circled the areola of one taut nipple then returned to Jonah's cock. "How do you want me?"

"I want you to move again."

"Sure?"

"*Yes.* Jesus would I say it if I wasn't?"

Trey focused, lifting them both so they stood straddling the cot, Jonah falling forward and Trey holding him in place, because he was shaking so much. Trey pulled out, almost out, felt the muscle to be giving and flexible, Jonah entirely used to his presence, and he plunged back in.

"Trey," Jonah breathed.

"God," said Trey as he withdrew, pushed in again, feeling the dark warm welcome. His body was flying, he never wanted it to end and he couldn't wait to reach the white fire that was coming. He pushed in a third and fourth time and Jonah's ass clenched him, his body rippling beneath Trey's, his lover coming again, and Trey could not stop, he kept moving even as his body seized with pleasure and he fell over into that timelessness when there was nothing but reaction and feeling.

He lost a moment there, not blacking out, but losing a certain awareness as he realized he was lying on top of a boneless Jonah with his full weight and he seemed incapable of doing anything about it. He didn't know if he could speak and his throat became uncomfortably full. As he thought about what he should do, Jonah squeezed him yet again, because Trey was still inside him, though slowly withdrawing.

Trey backed up, tried to stand and found his legs trembling. Turning over onto his back, Jonah looked up, solemn, and reached for Trey, pulling him into his embrace, pulling a sleeping bag over them both, taking both their full weights.

Trey had meant to be more graceful in the finishing of it, had meant to clean them both up and maybe talk about what happened. But his throat remained thick with emotion and his body lax and a little shaky in the after-throes of their lovemaking.

"We're going to sleep now," Jonah said, his voice deep and slurry, and he wrapped an arm around Trey's head, forcing him to use Jonah's shoulder as a pillow.

Trey did as he was told.

Chapter Ten

The next day was sharp and clean, bright blue, and they used it to wash everything, the freezing wind drying out the bedding and clothes in a surprisingly short time.

As the day progressed, the wind changed, increased, and the sky began to blur while the sun was setting.

"Another storm coming," Jonah declared, breathing in the smell of snow to come. Beside him, Trey nodded, scenting it too.

They stood outside, huddled together for warmth but wanting the fresh air. Jonah kissed Trey on the cheek and said, "I've never been so happy."

But it was a solemn declaration, not joyous like it might have been yesterday, when he'd been reeling, in the best way possible, by how Trey had loved him. Even now, thinking of how Trey had possessed him—and that's what it had felt like—made Jonah hard and needy and wanting. His body had discovered an entire new continent of sensation, and if he could have slowed down this desire and longing, Jonah wouldn't have. He felt like he had come alive, all because of Trey. But it would end, shortly, which made Jonah feel like his joy was balanced by the loss that was soon to come.

He wondered if Trey would respond to his declaration, because Trey's expression suggested he too was happy. But Trey took Jonah's hand and pulled him back inside. He didn't say a word as he undressed Jonah and they made love. Jonah had wanted to tell Trey to possess him again, but Trey wouldn't let him speak as he kissed and held and touched Jonah until they both came.

Afterwards, Jonah felt wide awake, not tired, and Trey laughed. "It never tires you out, does it?"

"You tired me out yesterday."

"That's true."

Jonah swallowed once. The vocabulary of this kind of conversation didn't come that easily to him. He kept his voice low. "You can take me like that again."

Trey reached up to smooth back the hair that was falling in Jonah's face. "Then I will."

Jonah was on top of Trey, pinning him down. He wanted to ask if he could fuck Trey sometime, but had to work his way up to that question. And he had other questions. Jonah bit his lip for moment before saying, "I guess twenty-four is pretty old for a first time."

Trey managed to shrug while lying horizontal. "There are people who wait longer." At Jonah's doubtful look, he added, "With werewolves it's probably less likely though."

"How old were you?"

Trey went still, and Jonah knew he didn't want to respond. He should have let him off the hook, but they were running out of time and he was hungry to know about this amazing man who lay beneath him. So he kept his gaze on Trey who appeared to feel he was obliged to answer. "I was twelve."

Something settled in Jonah, a feeling of dread, a need to brace himself, for Trey's sake. He worked not to look aghast. "That's a bit young," he managed, understating it.

"It was young," Trey agreed, no amending, no adding that he was mature for his age or something.

Jonah knew he was frowning. "Someone should have been looking out for you."

"I ran away from home at twelve, found a pack. It was a bit of a free-for-all during the week of the full moon."

Jonah kept his tone even. "Adults too?"

"Not usually, as that was frowned upon." Trey's eyes lidded. He didn't want to be talking about it. "I was willing, you have to understand. I wasn't dragged in to it kicking and screaming. The wolf wants a release during that time."

"Someone should have looked out for you," Jonah insisted, angry now that Trey hadn't had someone. He deserved to have someone like that. "I would have."

Trey laughed, though the humor was muted. "You weren't born then, Jonah."

"I wish I had been. I would have kept you safe."

Trey closed his eyes briefly, as if to escape Jonah's gaze, and Jonah thought Trey would kiss him to get away from the conversation. Instead he opened his eyes and quietly said, "I'm glad you're here now. More than you might realize."

Jonah lowered himself to rest his chin on Trey's chest. "Good."

Trey ruffled his hair. "Feeling sleepy now?"

He was a little surprised to realize this was true. He'd somehow expected a long conversation, but Trey's revelation—age *twelve*—had kind of cut it short. His eyes drifted shut as Trey rubbed a hand up and down his back. Being lulled to sleep was wonderful. But as Jonah's mind drifted, his thoughts circled back round to the point he'd made to Trey, though he switched it to present tense. *I will keep you safe.* It was silly in a way. Trey was capable, powerful and much more worldly than Jonah. And yet, it felt right to Jonah that part of his purpose in this world was to be there for Trey.

They started early the next day, and it wasn't Jonah making the first move though he was the one who often woke earlier. Of course Trey usually decided *what* they were doing. Not that Jonah was indecisive, exactly, more unsure and eager to follow Trey's lead. This morning he also wanted to ask Trey more questions, especially about his work, which he knew so little about, apart from the fact it was law enforcement and it was dangerous.

He wondered if he could talk Trey out of leaving. At first, the idea had been ludicrous. Why would Trey do any such thing for a virtual stranger? But as Trey's large palm skimmed up Jonah's inner thigh and held his balls, he couldn't help but feel that Trey wasn't like this with anyone else.

Jonah was already anticipating Trey touching his ass again. He spread his knees in invitation. But Trey took it as another kind of invitation and deep-throated Jonah.

Deep-throated. New word, thought Jonah rather blindly as the warm wetness of Trey's skillful mouth had his eyes rolling up into the back of his head.

He lifted his legs onto Trey's powerful shoulders. It was an invitation, except Trey didn't stop working Jonah's cock with his mouth. His tongue circled to the so-sensitive head, sliding over slit and around the edge before taking the length of him back into his mouth. Jonah couldn't possibly complain and the idea of being fucked receded as pleasure flooded through his body. They hadn't even kissed this morning and he was going to come and he didn't have the strength of mind to fight it.

Again Trey's tongue caressed Jonah's cock and all Jonah managed was to make his "ungghh" noise.

Just before he would have popped off, Trey lifted his head and said, "Touch your nipples."

"*What?*" He was naked and Trey was dressed, par for the course, but he didn't give a shit.

"Bring your fingers to your nipples and touch them as if they were mine."

Dumbly Jonah did, feeling a little self-conscious while Trey smiled and traced precome around Jonah's glans.

"Exactly. Perfect."

Jonah blushed at the praise, found himself reacting to his own touch as Trey blew softly over his wet cock.

"Keep going," Trey directed and Jonah obeyed, though it was soon hard to concentrate with Trey's mouth sucking him, hard now, Trey's hand cupping his sac, and finally Trey's finger tracing backward from Jonah's balls to his hole.

A guttural noise arose within him as that finger circled the muscle and Jonah was trembling, arching, when the finger slid home and he forgot what he was doing, just knew he was coming, Trey taking him higher by continuing to suck and lick while Jonah pumped out his come.

He was barely aware the finger had withdrawn, and then Trey too, going to wash hands while Jonah lay boneless across the cot.

Trey walked back, evidently still hard, and in a moment, Jonah planned to do something about that. He was still catching his breath.

Grinning down, Trey said, "I think you're getting the hang of this."

"You *think?*" Jonah felt like he'd taken to sex, or sex with Trey, like a duck to water. It was the most incredible discovery he'd ever made and it wasn't even a discovery but rather a creation between the two of them.

"Yeah." Trey bent over and cradled Jonah's face, stroking a thumb across his cheek. "You're so relaxed after sex now."

It was true. At first, his body had just wanted *more more more* and his mind couldn't settle down completely, wondering what might happen next. Jonah found himself beaming up at Trey, and he didn't care if he showed all his emotion on his face. "I'll recover."

"I know," said Trey wryly.

"And then we can take care of you."

"It doesn't have to be tit for tat, you know."

"That's not why. I like touching you. You like me touching you." Jonah tried not to sound defiant with that last statement, but it was true.

"You're right. I do."

Jonah licked his lips, wondering how to word his next question. Trey said sexual things easily, but somehow they sounded more awkward on Jonah's lips.

Trey slid in to sit beside him, traced Jonah's mouth with one finger. "Speak."

Jonah nipped the finger, as if for courage. "I'd like to fuck you."

Trey's eyes darkened, a sign of lust, Jonah knew, but it was somehow more complicated than that. Trey had also told Jonah that not every man liked everything and it was okay if he ever said no, or started stating preferences. Something Jonah had not yet been able to do because he'd loved everything Trey had done to him or he'd done to Trey or they'd done together.

"Okay," said Trey slowly.

"It's okay if you don't like being fucked. I just wanted to make you feel as good as you've made me feel."

"You already have." Trey was tracing a line down the center of Jonah's chest.

The next words came out of his mouth, seemingly of their

own volition. "Then stay with me. Don't leave."

Trey's gaze didn't veer away from Jonah's, but his finger stopped moving. His voice filled with regret when he said, "I can't."

"Why not?"

Trey's expression became impassive, almost stonelike.

Yet Jonah persisted. "I'm not saying you don't have reasons to leave, only that I'd like to understand them."

For a moment, he thought Trey was going to rise and walk away, and Jonah braced himself for the rebuff. Instead, Trey let out a long sigh as he fell onto the cot beside Jonah. He draped a leg across Jonah's hips and an arm across his chest, essentially imprisoning him.

"Look at me," Trey said, and Jonah turned his head on the pillow. While he'd wanted Trey's words, he accepted the kiss Trey gave him, accepted Trey's tongue tracing his lips, then delving in deep to steal his breath. Accepted then fought back, wanting more than to be trapped beneath Trey's steady, insistent and, Jonah recognized, passionate onslaught. Jonah was hard again and Trey encouraged him, his warm, strong hand stroking Jonah how he liked it.

Fine, thought Jonah, mind getting muzzy, throat making low guttural noises, *but I'll come again and then I'll ask again.*

Trey broke it off, and Jonah felt a little bereft, though he'd barely retreated. "I promised myself I'd answer your questions."

They were both breathing heavily and it would have been easy to thrust up into Trey's hand that still held him, to lean over and kiss Trey. But Jonah lay there, waiting.

"I work for the FBI."

Jonah's eyes widened and he might have softened, but with his words Trey kept a steady action on Jonah's cock, and he echoed, "FBI?"

Trey nodded, looking like he'd admitted to being part of the mafia or something.

"Wow." Then Jonah gasped a little as Trey ran fingertips over his sensitive sac.

Trey smiled down in that direction. "I'm sorry I can't resist touching you."

"I'm not complaining, as long as you keep"—Jonah yanked in a breath as Trey's thumb slid back and forth over his slit—"keep talking."

"I'm about to infiltrate another agency, one that has done a lot of damage to psychics."

Jonah snorted, despite the way Trey's hand kept working him. Rather breathily, he said, "Psychics? Come on."

"These people are called Minders and they have the ability to force their thoughts on others, force them to act in certain ways. They can be dangerous, but the agency is worse, dangerous to them and dangerous to anyone like us."

"But there are no psychics," Jonah protested.

Trey lifted an eyebrow. "Like there are no lynx shifters?"

"That's different."

Trey shook his head as he used Jonah's precome to lubricate his hand, pumping steadily. "They're going to go after shifters next, so I have to destroy this agency."

"They know about you?" Again, in his alarm, Jonah would have softened, but Trey took his slick finger and began tracing a circle around his hole. "*God.*"

"Do I have to stop?" Trey flicked a glance downward, and his hole felt so sensitive, so sexy, and Jonah had never known.

"No," Jonah gasped.

"You're addictive."

"*I'm* addictive?" His voice sounded high and thready and

incredulous. "You, this, is addictive."

"We like each other," Trey agreed.

"*Like,*" Jonah scoffed. "Such a mild word."

"An important word, even if it's more than that."

Jonah was going crazy with this touching, which he knew was part of Trey's plan. Trey was plainly uncomfortable talking about his work. *Focus, Jonah.* He clutched the bedding.

"Trey," he demanded, if a little unevenly. "Do they know about you?"

"No. I can keep my secret. I have good control, I've told you."

"Too good."

Trey grinned. "I love the way you respond to me."

"I'm actually worried about you."

Trey slid in his finger and Jonah groaned as Trey massaged...just...that...spot.

"Trey, I'm going to come."

"Soon," he agreed.

"I want you to come."

"I thought you wanted to fuck me."

Jonah's mouth opened in an O and Trey swooped down. This time he battled for the kiss as Trey stretched him with two fingers, as his body tightened, preparing for his release. Jonah fought to hold his own in the kiss and the fire flooded through him, taking the fight away as he spurted, splattering on his own belly, his body accepting Trey's deep kiss and Trey's strong, clever fingers.

Trey didn't stop right away as if he was stretching out Jonah's orgasm as long as possible, and only when Jonah was completely lax did Trey withdraw.

His eyes crinkled, warm and loving, his face open and smiling, and this was perhaps his greatest gift to Jonah. Or so Jonah thought until Trey said, "Do you really want me?"

Though Jonah felt boneless, all tension gone, he nodded, because the offer sent a thrill through him, and he knew he would tighten with passion in no time at all. "You have to make sure I don't hurt you."

Trey's eyelids went to half-mast. "I can do that."

Chapter Eleven

Jonah found he was more nervous now than at any time since before Trey had made it clear he was interested in Jonah sexually. He watched Trey move, all muscle beneath the too-tight clothing, Jonah's clothing, that he wore. He declared it his turn to stoke the fire and heat the food, told Jonah to keep warm.

As if sensing his nervousness, Trey glanced over at Jonah. "You need to eat a bit more. You're on the thin side."

"I've always been."

Trey inclined his head in acknowledgment. "It can be dangerous for a shifter, given the way we can use our resources too quickly and become weak."

Jonah had noted that Trey ate with due diligence more than gusto but had put that down to him not being terribly enthusiastic about the food supply here.

"I'll try to eat more," Jonah offered.

"Good."

They settled on the cot, facing each other as they ate out of the wooden bowls his mother had carved all those years ago. He should try to focus on her good points more, what she'd set up for him here, how she'd loved him. But sometimes, her inadequacies overwhelmed the better memories. She'd been unable to keep shitty men out of her life, and she'd favored him over Craig. You couldn't say such favoritism had led to Craig's death, but Craig's anger and stupidity had been driven in part by his dysfunctional family.

"Who are you thinking about?"

Jonah sighed. He hadn't wanted his mind wandering this way, not when they were running out of time, but that was why of course. Craig had left him by dying, though, and at least Trey wasn't doing that. "My brother."

Quiet-faced, Trey asked, "Did you find him?"

Jonah closed his eyes on a nod. "He got lost in a blizzard. He shouldn't have gone out." He jerked his head towards the door that led outside. "The weather was like today's, a storm calling. He got pissed off at me and I let him go, he was so angry. I thought I could find him before it was too late. I didn't even wait that long to follow him. But I was wrong."

"I'm so sorry." Trey's gaze wasn't pity so much as fellow-feeling.

"I failed Craig. So did my mother. It was very hard on him, this kind of life." Jonah was worried Trey would tell him Craig had chosen to go out in that blizzard, and he didn't want to hear it.

But Trey just quirked his mouth, more commiseration than humor. "This life is hard." With a sigh, he added, "I failed my brother. Left him when he was a toddler, when he adored me, left him to my asshole father. My brother never forgave me."

"You were twelve."

Trey lifted one shoulder and let it drop. Jonah was tempted to say it wasn't his fault, he'd been a child himself and unable to care for another child, but he hadn't wanted such assurances from Trey so he held his tongue.

"I leave people," Trey continued, "and they become damaged or they die." He gazed directly at Jonah. "You mustn't

121

do that. You wait here for me and I'll come back."

Jonah could wait, and the idea that it was important to Trey that he stay here made his chest tight with hope and pain. The waiting was not going to be easy. Still, he nodded. "As long as you don't die, it's a deal."

"I'm a shifter. I won't freeze in this blizzard or another."

"There are other ways to die." Jonah didn't like the sounds of Trey's FBI work.

"Don't worry, I'm good at my job."

This time Jonah liked to hear Trey's arrogance, he made it sound true.

As he washed the dishes, Jonah's tension returned, and he wasn't sure if it was because Trey was leaving or because he felt a little at sea about this next step.

Trey's arms came around him from behind, one over his shoulder, one under the other, locking his back to Trey's chest in a way that made him feel very secure. Trey's erection pressed against Jonah's backside.

"You don't have to do anything you don't want," Trey murmured. "You know that, right?"

"I know." Jonah rubbed against Trey, his touch making Jonah relax. "You haven't come today."

"I will. I'm a little older, I have to conserve my energy."

Privately Jonah thought it might have something to do with the fact that Trey wasn't quite so absolutely enthralled by Jonah as Jonah was with Trey. But as Trey mouthed the tendon at the juncture of his neck and shoulder, Jonah knew that Trey cared, knew that Trey had a hard time not touching him. And that counted for something, maybe for a lot. It was a bit hard judging these things, given his total lack of experience. Jonah just had to believe.

"So much thinking," Trey observed. "Hard to feel when you think too much."

Jonah let out a full-body sigh as his dick hardened, coming to attention. "Hard not to think when you're leaving."

"I know." Trey took him by the hand and tugged him over to the cot. Quickly, almost dispassionately except for the intensity of his gaze, he undressed Jonah and himself, then lay down. At Jonah's frown, he smiled up. "You needn't worry. I'm easy."

Jonah wasn't entirely sure what Trey meant but decided that if in doubt, kissing was the best thing. So he went to Trey, nuzzled his cheek and kissed, waiting for Trey to take over. When he didn't Jonah went further, kissing harder, demanding a response until Trey's hand was fisting Jonah's hair while his other arm banded across Jonah's back, holding him tight, taking Jonah's breath, overwhelming him in all the right ways.

They rubbed against each other, finding friction, finding a rhythm. Jonah wasn't sure how long it went on, though it was beautiful, beautiful and simple, and then Trey was groaning, arching his back under him, coming against their bellies.

Jonah kept kissing, though Trey's fight had gone out of him with his orgasm. His mouth was still warm and welcoming and tender, as if he could kiss like this forever, but he let Jonah control it. Finally Jonah broke off, heaved a breath and realized he was beaming down at Trey. "You came before me."

Trey's eyes were dark as midnight, except for a thin iris of blue. "Stay there," he said, his words slightly slurred as he used his own come to slick Jonah's penis. "Do you still want to come inside me?"

Jonah nodded once.

"I am very relaxed. You're not going to hurt me. Okay?"

Again Jonah nodded.

With that, Trey shifted Jonah back and Jonah assumed he would turn around, but instead he lifted his powerful legs onto Jonah's shoulders. They remained facing each other as Jonah was positioned at Trey's entrance. "Move forward."

Tentatively, Jonah pressed against Trey's hole, worried, remembering how long Trey had worked him before he'd actually thrust inside.

"We're all different. Trust me."

Jonah pushed and Trey opened up, the circle of muscle tight but giving as his head entered Trey. "Okay?" he said thickly, overcome by how incredible this felt, trying not to lose it here and now. The muscle's strong grip was about to pull him over the edge.

Trey grinned and shifted downwards, and Jonah pushed forward all the way in at once. The warmth, the powerful, sure hold of Trey, the sensation of coming home—Jonah's entire body seized. "Trey?"

"I've got you."

He panted, trying not to lose it in the next second. He managed to grit out, "I can't… I'm going to…"

"Do it. Just stay with me." Trey caressed Jonah's cheek and Jonah turned his face into the palm, a kiss that managed to take him away from the edge.

He pulled out, pushed in again, his eyes rolling back in his effort to make this last. But the third time he stroked into Trey was the last, as he ejaculated before he wanted to, and he was almost sobbing with need even as that need was being answered.

He'd wanted it to last longer. He managed to say as much while Trey held him in his arms, murmuring that Jonah was beautiful and wonderful and exactly what he wanted.

Jonah buried himself in Trey's neck, breathing shakily, and

he didn't know if it was because it was the first time he'd been inside Trey or because it was last.

Soon Trey would be gone.

Suddenly Jonah felt exhausted, the tension between learning so much about his body, about Trey's body, about what they could be together, and knowing they would not see each other again for a long, long time. So Jonah closed his eyes against Trey's skin and listened to his lover comfort him with words of praise and words of affection, and with promises that he'd return to Jonah.

He fell asleep, dimly aware that Trey was rising to clean up, himself and Jonah. And when Trey said, "I'll be back," Jonah fell into deeper sleep.

Much later he woke to an empty hut and a dead fire. He didn't know how long he'd slept, but the emptiness, the loneliness of his home, shocked him.

He hadn't imagined those words would be Trey's final goodbye. Jonah hadn't even answered them.

Pushing himself to sitting in the frigid room, he took his naked body to the door and opened it. Welcomed the sharp, painful cold that assaulted him even as he observed that it wasn't boot prints that had left his sheltered cave, but paw prints. Wolf tracks that disappeared into a storm that was sweeping everything away. A curtain of snow was falling across the cave's opening.

It was as if Trey had wanted to make double sure Jonah wouldn't try to follow him.

He stood there for a while, until his entire body juddered with the cold, until his skin threatened to slowly die of frostbite. Then he made the decision not to punish himself further and retreated inside, got dressed, started a fire. He had promised Trey he'd eat more, so he did. Trey had promised Jonah he would return, and Jonah believed he would. All he could do now was wait.

Trey ran, through the snow, through the cold. The exhilaration of four weeks ago, when he'd discovered something or someone had begun to track him, was completely gone. That had been the start of his relationship with Jonah and this abrupt leave-taking was the end. He felt like he was returning to hell while abandoning someone who depended on him.

He'd abandoned two-year-old Gabriel, and his brother had grown into a violent, murderous adult. He'd abandoned Quinn for a two-week job and returned to find his lover's body ripped apart by wolves. And now he was leaving Jonah behind. But Jonah was not a toddler with an abusive father, and neither wolves nor FBI knew of Jonah's home, let alone his existence.

This time Trey would return and Jonah would be there for him, healthy and whole, if a little angry, perhaps. It was hard to be the one left behind, but Jonah would be alive because no one but Trey knew about him. Being alive counted for something, counted for a lot.

Two and half days and many snowy miles later, Trey returned to his car parked in the abandoned hangar, exactly where he'd left it. Inside the trunk were his clothes and winter gear. No one, as far as Trey could tell, had been here over the past month. The only scent he smelled was his own. It was safe to turn human.

So he lay down beside the vehicle and threw himself almost violently into the shift, then woke to mild panic and the realization that he needed to stand up, get out of the snow, open the car door and get properly dressed. Having not eaten since he'd left Jonah, Trey was ravenous and he ripped into his protein bars. He was thirsty too, but had to wait and guzzle water after the bottles had been melted by the car's heater.

126

By then he was on the road, heading south, heading back to his work. Moving far, far away from Jonah who was safer without him, at least for now. Trey would destroy the rogue agency, make the world safer for shifters, including Jonah, and then he would return to find the only lynx he'd ever met. *His* lynx.

Chapter Twelve

Over the next year and a half of interminable waiting, Jonah proved himself wrong. He'd been confident, after the first shock of Trey's leaving, that he'd learn how to wait and Trey would return to him. But the waiting got more difficult not easier as time passed and passed, and what he learned was that patience is not always rewarded.

Eventually he learned that he could not outlast the long wait. He'd been through one entire, long winter alone and to face another was impossible, not without knowing what had happened to Trey.

As he packed up that fall he figured, with a kind of cold dullness that had taken him over, they had both broken their promises to each other. Eighteen months had passed—Trey had never returned and Jonah was no longer waiting. Instead he made the decision to go in search of the wolf who worked for the FBI.

He suspected Trey might never forgive him for seeking him out, for the wolf had made it clear it wasn't Jonah's role to find him. It was only Jonah's role to wait. However, Jonah didn't think he'd be able to forgive Trey for abandoning him.

If, indeed, that had happened. There was, in the end, one thing Jonah needed to discover—and dreaded to discover—whether or not Trey was dead.

For either Trey had died, or Trey had broken faith with him.

Going in, Trey had known Kingley would be his handler, and he'd wanted it no other way. Because Kingley would let certain things slide, would trade on ignorance in one area for knowledge in another, would sometimes trade unpalatable favors—for Trey was an excellent assassin and Kingley depended on him. It wasn't ethical, but Trey couldn't risk working with an ethical handler who might have kept a closer eye on what he was actually doing. Kingley didn't care, he just wanted results.

And Trey got them, the results. It didn't take all that long to infiltrate and become trusted by them—be trusted by Horton the asshole who ran the whole shitty anti-psychic agency. After all, Trey was a well-respected FBI agent. It didn't take all that long for Trey to locate a Minder who would eventually bring about the downfall of the agency. But despite his good work, reporting to Kingley in the year that followed became a dangerous dance.

Because Kingley had become interested in, as he called it, Trey's venture up north. While he'd been impassive, hadn't revealed a thing, it had actually been hard to breathe, thinking that Kingley could somehow know about Jonah.

He didn't, not really. But Kingley had known that Trey'd been in the general vicinity of a few odd reports. A few deaths by wolves, something Trey feared was due to his brother's violent activities. And a few reports of strange animal sightings in a city where Trey's nephew lived.

The upshot was that Kingley remained on high alert about Trey's true nature. So instead of returning to Jonah that first summer as he'd wanted, Trey stayed put. He could not risk piquing Kingley's interest, pointing him towards Jonah's safe harbor. Trey's heart ached, it was a strangely physical pain, and Trey didn't know quite what to do with it except throw himself into work. As time passed and events within the agency became more interesting—an escaped Minder for one—Kingley's interest in Trey's other nature, and in his trip up into the Canadian Shield, seemed to abate.

So two years later, again in the dead of winter, though this time without a snowstorm, Trey managed to disappear off Kingley's radar and he felt safe enough to turn himself wolf and head north towards Jonah's. There was exhilaration in him, he couldn't deny it, but it was accompanied by a minor chord of dread. A two years' absence was going to be hard to explain, and harder to forgive.

For quite a while, Trey turned over the possibilities in his mind, trying to describe to Jonah what had happened to keep him away. That Kingley was a threat, that Horton his faux-boss was also someone who kept too close an eye on him. Trey had been protecting Jonah, that was clear to Trey, but it would be harder to convince a hermit lynx who had little to do with humans. Over two years Jonah's trust would have eroded, especially when Trey had asked him to wait for a year and not much more. He'd never dreamed he'd be away this long.

He should have known better.

Distracted by his thoughts and fears, Trey didn't immediately realize he had reached the huge rock face that sheltered Jonah's home.

In part because he was surprised to find no hint of Jonah's existence—no scent, no sound, no snowshoe paw prints.

Trey's heart beat harder, in distress, though perhaps he was overreacting and Jonah had simply avoided venturing south of his cave. It was possible, but odd, and Trey's dread rose as he pushed himself into a run, despite the fact he'd almost reached the limit of his endurance.

He broke into the clearing only to see the cave filled with snow, a small drift having accumulated in its doorway, with no evidence of anyone traversing it to enter the house.

Trey stumbled then, his front legs collapsing for a moment before he forced himself to rise, his human panicking as his wolf took over completely.

He climbed over the mound of snow, noted its accumulation in the cave, noted the untouched wood stockpiled for winter, even as he kept moving for the inner door, lifting his paw to push down on the door handle's lever.

For five seconds he paused, opened his mouth and breathed in as deeply as possible. Smelled nothing. The scent of death didn't exist but it couldn't anyway, not in this freezing weather.

Gabriel flashed before his eyes. As did Quinn's ragged body. Fifteen years ago, Trey had walked through the door to his and Quinn's shared apartment, and walked into a life where Gabriel was lost to him and Quinn was utterly destroyed. Today was Jonah's turn to be ruined.

The paw pushed down. Trey shouldered into the house.

A small amount of sun filtered dimly through the skylight, enough for Trey to see that Jonah's body was not frozen in the main room. In fact, everything looked tidy, if unused. The dishes had been washed up, the fireplace cleaned, the bed made.

It gave him an odd kind of hope and enough courage to move on to the back room.

Also empty of Jonah. Trey nosed through his belongings, catching a faint whiff of Jonah's scent. His winter gear remained. So Jonah had left in warmer weather, or he'd left as lynx.

Despite the house being small, and Trey's nose being keen,

he made himself explore every nook and cranny, as if that would tell him something about Jonah's departure.

It didn't.

The light was failing now, as was he. His energy was gone, sapped, and part of him wanted to lie down on one of the two cots—his chest ached to see that Jonah had kept the two cots out—and never wake up again. He should eat, he knew he should. He'd never been so weak as to not eat to keep his strength up. It was why he remained strong.

But this time something in Trey gave. He didn't climb onto a cot. Instead he curled up on that rug he'd slept on as wolf those two long years ago, and he let himself fall into the oblivion of exhausted, painful sleep.

Trey woke in the dark and cold. As he breathed in, he recognized that Jonah's scent was close to nonexistent, a hint of it left in the rug and bedding, perhaps, if Trey allowed his imagination to go to work. But clearly Jonah had left here a while ago.

He didn't know if it made it better or worse, that Jonah was long gone. Trey hoped he'd left under his own steam, made the choice to go elsewhere.

Which was what Trey should do, simply leave. There was nothing he could accomplish here but the idea of going away again... He balked. Instead, Trey lay down and pushed himself to shift to human. His body resisted—the freezing temperatures and the full moon wanted him to remain wolf—so the pain was worse than usual. And Trey embraced that pain, anything to chase away the sadness that threatened to envelop him.

He woke a second time. His internal clock said it was half an hour later, long for him. The cold air didn't harm him, his body too heated by the shift. But that would change quickly.

While he was not in the best state of mind, he wasn't suicidal, so he strode to the back room and donned some of Jonah's clothes, then went to the fireplace to build a fire. Jonah had been organized in his leave-taking—matches still there and some supply of firewood, perhaps so if he returned in the dead of winter he could do as Trey was now doing.

During the two weeks that followed, Trey lived at Jonah's. He knew it was foolish to hope Jonah would arrive there unexpectedly, but he allowed himself the hope because otherwise it was hard to get through the day, to be around Jonah's things with Jonah himself absent.

He should have left immediately, of course. But if he lived here, went through the routine Jonah had gone through, maybe he could find some clue as to where Jonah had gone.

He refused to believe Jonah was dead. During his time in the cave, Trey searched the surrounding area, though admittedly the snow covered too much for the search to be as thorough as needed. He also was careful not to delve too deeply into the food supplies, in case Jonah arrived back a week after Trey left and needed them. Trey built up the firewood supply, cutting down trees, chopping up the wood.

And he wrote Jonah a long, long letter. He was careful with it, he didn't put down his name, or Jonah's, but he made it clear that he'd been here and why he'd been away. And he promised to return midsummer, having reason to believe he could safely get away then.

The letter writing brought him no pleasure, it was painful from beginning to end, but he owed Jonah that much.

The day Trey left the sun was shining, the hard light assaulted his eyes and the hard snow cut his paws on his way out. Despite the danger of it, Trey went to the nearby town where Jonah had picked up supplies, and asked some questions.

A couple of people recalled that Jonah had been in their store—it was notable since the strange young man used only cash for purchases and acted uneasy. *Weird*, one of them said in describing Jonah. But no one had actually seen him since last June.

Trouble was, like Trey himself, Jonah was a shifter. He'd disappeared from society but where he'd ended up was impossible to trace without a human trail or a lynx's scent. And Trey could find neither.

For the first few months after he left home, Jonah just learned how to get in and out of human society. Of course, he'd been into town before, but it had always been the same town, and he'd interacted with few people.

The first time he ventured into a city, albeit a small city, he frightened people with his unclean clothes and his unshaved face. It was technically difficult to travel this way, as lynx, and emerge as human in the cities. Trey had mentioned that some shifters, moving back and forth between forms, ended up stealing clothes and though he hated it, Jonah snatched some clothes hanging on a line from time to time. They weren't always easy to find in the late fall.

He ended up being picked up by police on his third attempt to enter a city. Aaron had declared all police assholes, something that had influenced Jonah no matter how much he hated Aaron. But these men were concerned by Jonah's inability to answer basic questions or show them any ID. His mother had never registered him for any, so his name was truthful when he said Jonah.

He landed in a homeless shelter where he was given

clothes, food, shaving supplies. He'd expected to find it difficult to be among so many people, and it was. And yet, there was a relief in him, to not be so alone all the time. After Trey had left, the solitude had become more oppressive, and it had been bad before.

Jonah wasn't terribly communicative, and he couldn't last too long at one shelter, because he had to leave off and go lynx for a while, recover from all the socialization. But a year after he'd left home, he'd created a circuit for himself in three cities, at three different shelters, leaving caches of clothing for when he'd shift back to human.

He tried working from time to time, under the table it was called, but people tended to cheat him or he couldn't stand the long hours and the restlessness that induced. Recognizing he wasn't cut out for human society wasn't the most welcome truth, but he accepted it as he accepted most things these days.

The only thing that kept him from becoming entirely listless and dull about life was his search for Trey. He'd asked at a few police stations about Trey Walters. The first couple of times he'd feared that he would learn that Trey had been killed in some kind of FBI-related fieldwork.

But no one knew anything, when they bothered to take his query seriously. A couple of people dug deeper and told him Trey had lied, that no Trey Walters had ever worked for the FBI. Jonah tossed that idea around in his head, that Trey and everything he'd said was bogus. Thing was, as Jonah spent more and more time around humans, he'd begun to pick up signals that they were lying, signals associated with sight and smell. And Trey had seemed to be speaking truth, at least in Jonah's memories—if they could be depended on.

Then one morning, a cop came to find Jonah. It was spring, more than a year and a half after he'd left home, and he was thinking he might take a reprieve and return there soon. That morning, Jonah was actually working, paving driveways. The smell on the job was atrocious, and the job wasn't going to last long, but there was something satisfying about working in society. He planned to leave the money at the shelter since he couldn't take it with him. Though they didn't appreciate such gestures and believed them to be counterproductive, because they wanted him to build a life.

"Jonah?"

Jonah recognized the cop and nodded before they shook hands. This guy liked Jonah okay. The cop tilted his head to the right to indicate an older man, dressed casually, who stood off to the side, across the road from where they were working on this driveway.

Jonah raised his eyebrows in question and the cop, Neil was his name if he remembered correctly, gave him a brief clap on the back while Jonah forced himself not to flinch. Despite all his human interactions, he wasn't used to physical contact and didn't particularly appreciate it, even if it was meant to be reassuring.

"Don't worry, you're not in trouble." Neil started walking and Jonah obediently fell in step. "Remember you were asking about a Trey Walters?"

Jonah faltered briefly and tried not to react in an obvious manner. Humans thought there was something wrong with him when he revealed too much emotion. But of course he remembered.

"I found someone who might be able to answer some of your questions."

And then they were there, across the road, Jonah staring into the pale eyes of a middle-aged man with a grizzled beard. Jonah had the impression FBI agents were likely to be clean-shaven and tried not to show his disappointment. After all this time, it seemed impossible to think this nondescript man might know something about Trey. Still, Jonah kept a tight grip on himself, because the speculative look in the stranger's eyes made him uneasy. In addition there was a scent about him that Jonah had come to associate with anticipation.

The bearded man was excited to be meeting Jonah.

"Jonah Carvin," he said, introducing himself and putting out his hand. Taking the initiative sometimes helped him in situations where he couldn't predict what would happen next.

The man didn't smile, just gave Jonah the briefest once-over, an assessment of sorts, before putting out his hand in return. As they shook, he said, "My name is Horton. I wanted to ask you some questions about Trey Walters."

Jonah's throat felt dry but he forced the words out. "Is he alive?"

"Absolutely. But I'm surprised that you've met him. And that's what we have to talk about."

"All right," Jonah said slowly and looked once to Neil, for reassurance, he supposed, though how the cop could reassure him, Jonah didn't know.

"We'll go back to the station." Neil indicated the police car. "You're not in trouble."

"Not at all," Horton added smoothly, causing the back of Jonah's neck to prickle, invisible cat fur rising in distrust. Nevertheless, his desire to hear more about Trey trumped his reluctance to be with this man, so Jonah collected his belongings, explained the situation to his boss and slid into the backseat of the police car.

Chapter Thirteen

Jonah woke to a blurred hazy world. He was finally back at home, in his cot.

No, not at home. Why had he thought that? He lay on a bed, on a mattress. There were lines surrounding him. Bars?

That couldn't be right. He blinked more than a few times, though his eyelids were heavy and it was difficult to see. There were bars on the bed. Bars at the door. When he tried to lift his head, its weight held him down and that alarmed him so much that he forced himself to sit up. The room spun, and he felt himself collapsing as his world turned black.

His lynx wanted to escape. That's all he knew as he faded in and out of consciousness. But he lay plastered to the bed, unable to move, still human and without enough energy to rise despite his lynx raging within.

He wasn't always alone.

"Jonah," said the voice. It had spoken before, and the only thing Jonah could do was pretend it didn't exist. He wasn't thinking coherently enough to know why he should keep up this show of pretense, but it took no energy and it seemed to be the safest option. He followed his cat's instinct.

"Jonah Carvin." A more authoritative tone this time. "You do not have enough drug in your body to be this incapacitated.

I've tested you people. A wolf would have shifted by now and be pacing your cell."

Good thing I'm not a wolf.

"So wolf means something to you, does it?" A soft grunt. The voice had expected a reaction and he got one, though Jonah didn't know what he'd done, what he'd revealed.

Wolf meant Trey, but Jonah intended to say nothing about Trey. In fact, he thought he might never speak again. Certainly not under these conditions. The voice repeated his name and other nonsensical words followed. The voice was commanding, directing, but Jonah did not bother to listen, to decipher the flow of the words. He let the noise pass by him and allowed himself to fall back into the abyss.

The next time he woke, he was bound—shackled tightly around one wrist and one ankle so that he could not shift to escape—but at least his head had cleared.

"Are you human?" That voice again, Jonah was getting tired of it and he hadn't been conscious for all that long over the past few...days? His internal clock said it was possible a week had passed. Drugs made his estimate fuzzy.

This time a hand came out and shook Jonah's shoulder. He flinched and the hand lifted off him.

"Open your eyes and look at me."

Jonah didn't really see the point.

The man swore. "What the fuck? There is no way in hell you're a wolf."

This time Jonah made the effort not to react, and succeeded. Who was this asshole?

"Okay, Jonah, here's how it's going to be. There's no IV, not any longer"—at which point Jonah vaguely recalled there'd been something in his arm while he'd drifted in and out of consciousness—"so you're going to get damned thirsty if I don't give you something to drink."

Hmmm. Dying of thirst wasn't the most appealing thing Jonah had heard of. Then again, he wasn't feeling very tractable at the moment.

"I can't fucking believe it. Christ." The man heaved another breath as if he were running a race, or was hugely disappointed. Jonah became curious. He'd never disappointed anyone to this extent for so little reason, and this guy was a perfect stranger.

He opened his eyes, turned his head. Stared into the face of a man he now remembered—Horton. Neil the cop had introduced them and left them in a room together to talk. Last thing Jonah remembered he'd taken a drink of water.

He hoped Neil didn't feel too badly. The cop had liked to look out for Jonah, had believed he was doing Jonah a favor by bringing Horton to him.

"Okay, reward time. You did as you were told. You get a drink." Horton didn't sound enthusiastic about Jonah's "reward".

Jonah swallowed, noting his throat was dry, before he spoke. "Why are you talking to me about wolves?"

More swearing, not particularly colorful. Well, this had to be the most unusual experience of Jonah's life, being shackled to a bed and disappointing some man because he wasn't a werewolf.

"Do I get a drink?"

The man didn't move, but his expression changed then, and Jonah realized he was being perceived as useless. He wondered in a rather theoretical way if he was going to be killed. This thought didn't alarm him, and whether that was the leftover effects of the drugs that had been in his body for a week or simply the dullness that had invaded his thinking over the past year, he didn't know.

However, instead of slitting Jonah's throat or whatever other means of murder the man would have used, he passed Jonah a bottle of water which he took with his free hand.

Rising awkwardly given his shackles, Jonah tipped back his head and drank deeply, only then realizing he was hungry. Whether it was wise to admit it or not, he didn't know. The expression on the man's face was changing again, disappointment still evident, but also a speculative look.

"How well did you know Trey?"

Jonah stared straight ahead. He didn't want to speak of Trey to anyone, ever. Trey was dead, or Trey had broken an important promise to Jonah, something he was not going to be able to forgive him for. Either way, Horton obviously knew something about Trey's link to werewolves and Jonah refused to give Trey away to his captor. He couldn't stand the idea of Trey being held by Horton in this manner.

His stomach rumbled and Horton threatened again. "Answer my questions or your skinny body is going to get skinnier."

Lifting one shoulder in a slight shrug, Jonah drank more.

"I cannot understand what Trey would be doing with a homeless human. Homeless wolf, sure. Not human. And you're sure as hell not one of those rare cougars or you'd be a snarling mess."

Jonah smiled. He wasn't a cougar, no. He supposed lynxes were less aggressive. But they knew how to go after prey. When Aaron had beat his mother once too often and too hard and she never woke up again, Jonah had bided his time before becoming the predator and ripping out Aaron's throat. Jonah was beginning to think he would stalk Horton too, though it was going to be trickier, given that he was bound to this bed and Horton was a free man.

"How did you meet Trey?" Horton asked.

To stalk someone, you sometimes had to interact with them, so Jonah cocked his head, considering his words. "He told me he'd come back."

"That's not an answer, Jonah."

"But you came instead." Here, Jonah met Horton's pale blue gaze. "You're a liar, so it's pointless to say much to you."

Horton frowned. "I haven't lied to you."

"You misrepresented yourself to Neil. He wouldn't have wanted you to kidnap and drug me." Jonah thought he sounded quite reasonable given the situation, but Horton appeared annoyed by his logic.

The man proceeded to speak to Jonah as if he were a simpleton. Just as well. Best to be underestimated. "What you don't understand, Jonah, is that Trey is a dangerous man."

So Trey lived, or Horton believed he did, and despite all his anger, this idea made something within Jonah rise, become alive. While he could never be with Trey again, he wanted to see him one last time, a kind of goodbye.

"If you lie to me, there's not much point in us talking. It's a problem for me," Jonah said.

Horton rolled his eyes. "Do you want to get food or not, Jonah? That's what you should be most concerned about, not my *lying.*" He smiled, an ugly expression. "I'm not the one who's chained to the bed here, Jonah."

He gritted his teeth at the way Horton kept repeating his name. "Problem is, I can't trust you to give food to me one way or the other. Also? I don't have much information to give you."

"Trey was looking for you, Jonah."

He couldn't help himself. He glanced at Horton and sensed truth.

"And you care about that." Horton bent forward, clearly satisfied by Jonah's reaction. "So you are lucky today. You will be useful to me. This means you have a future."

Jonah was supposed to be cowed by Horton holding his life in his hands. And two years ago, he would have been. But now something had broken and all Jonah cared about was stalking Horton to the bitter end. It had been this way with Aaron too. The stalking and killing of that man had, for better or worse, blunted his grief at losing his mother. Now he'd lost Trey and Horton's death would be his way of saying goodbye. Trey would be safer with Horton dead. Despite everything, Jonah wanted to keep Trey safe.

Jonah wondered if he could convince Horton to come close enough for him to grab the man's throat. He'd been weakened by the past week, yes, but he was still stronger than the normal human.

"A few rules, Jonah. If you make any move to harm me at any point you will be restrained again, and indefinitely. Also, if I decide you are actually useless to me and have no useful knowledge of Trey, you will regret it." Here Horton smiled. "And you will die."

"You're a killer then." Jonah bared his teeth, but didn't add, *Like me.*

Horton was taken aback by this bald statement or perhaps by Jonah's lack of fear. "It's never my first choice."

Jonah wasn't going to feel bad when he killed this man. But he was also not going to do anything precipitous. He wanted to learn more about Trey before this was over. Also, and this was probably a bit warped, but he'd been isolated in a lot of ways during his life, and this situation was a new one. More onerous than before, with fewer freedoms, but the threat and the danger and general assholery of Horton had managed to dispel a little of the depressive feelings he'd been carrying with him for too long. There was challenge here, even if he failed to meet it.

"Are you understanding anything I'm telling you, Jonah?"

"I believe so."

"Your lack of affect is a bit...odd."

"I've been told that before." Only in the last two years actually, but Jonah thought of it as growing up and learning about the wider world.

With that, Horton unshackled Jonah completely and Jonah didn't attack. Horton wasn't a big man, but he was clearly in good physical shape and probably expected that in a physical match he could overpower a weakened Jonah. Well, the lynx in him could wait. One thing he'd discovered during his time with humans was how patient his lynx could be. He could be grateful he wasn't a wolf who needed to run during the full moon.

"I have one request." Jonah cleared his throat because this was important to him and his sanity, though Horton acceding to his request was unlikely. "I'd like to study math."

Incomprehension gave way to wariness. "Is that a joke?"

"No. I've always wanted to study math at the university level but didn't get the opportunity."

"Uh-huh." Horton had no interest in this revelation. Well, Jonah could ask again later. He hadn't expected an immediate yes.

"Trey was impressed by my interest in math," Jonah offered, a reward of sorts that couldn't hurt Trey, he didn't think.

"Really. Trey is never impressed by anything so I find that

hard to believe."

"I'm not the liar."

"When would he have told you that?" demanded Horton.

"When we met."

"Where was that?"

"At the library." Jonah didn't pause with that reply. There had been former library books in his house.

Horton just rolled his eyes.

"It keeps me sane. Do you want me sane, Horton?"

The man's look was assessing but his words dismissive. "I'll take it under consideration."

Time passed. Time Jonah mostly spent alone in a small space. At first he assumed he was being watched, but he soon came to realize his bigger danger was being forgotten. Of course there was no math, and no real interest by Horton. Sometimes it was Horton, sometimes it was a guard who wouldn't speak to Jonah, who came to deliver food, drink and basic toiletries.

The water was always cold and he was being held in a basement, no windows. Though he longed to turn cat, he wouldn't do it here. If they discovered he was a shifter, he would never escape. So his lynx waited and Jonah tried to keep up his strength even if they didn't feed him enough calories.

While Jonah's internal clock did work, he seemed barely aware of the months passing.

Then one day, Horton returned, excited and as interested in Jonah as he had been that first day. He snapped a picture of Jonah.

"A little pale and thin, but you're okay."

Jonah didn't react. He'd stopped reacting to Horton early on when it became clear it wouldn't help him. But now, suddenly, Horton appeared concerned by Jonah's health.

"Math, right?" he asked.

Jonah eyed him and said, not for the first time, "First-year university calculus and algebra. The books I used before are old and might be out of date."

Instead of appearing amused at his request, Horton nodded. "I'll get you textbooks. We need to get you some fresh air. You're looking a little washed out, too thin."

"I look like a prisoner?" Jonah asked mildly. "Who are you trying to impress?"

"Manipulate," Horton corrected. "We'll improve your conditions the more he cooperates."

Jonah waited.

"Trey will be angry with me if he thinks you've suffered overmuch."

Something in Jonah's heart ached to hear that. He was careful not to voice his doubts. His doubts weren't what this was about. If it was all about him, he'd stand up, cross the room and snap Horton's neck. But he wanted to warn Trey off this man first.

So he asked, "What do you want from Trey?"

Horton leveled his gaze at him and the expression was avid, but not in a murderous way. And yet what he said was "His blood."

Chapter Fourteen

Once the agency dug its claws in you, you were never entirely free. So though Trey's job was done and Horton was supposed to be in prison, he wasn't surprised to hear from the man a couple of months later. Horton had been released. He was free. Strings pulled and all that. Probably by Kingley, who'd wanted Horton's agency destroyed, but also wanted Horton in his debt.

By the end of his assignment, Trey had decided to disappear, couldn't handle being part of any agency any longer, be it FBI or the corrupt one he'd helped bring down. He had his own agenda—and number one on that list was to search for Jonah again. No longer constrained by his job, Trey was going to go about the search differently.

His biggest and most unrealistic hope had been that Jonah had returned home, was living there safe and sane. But this summer, as last, Jonah's cave had been empty, with no signs of Jonah having ever returned.

Trey worried Jonah was dead, though he refused to give up hope yet, for Jonah's sake if nothing else. So he was going to search in depth and see what he could find. Like assassination, he was good at it. And he preferred finding people to killing them.

But first, *Dan* Horton. Dan liked them to be on a first-name basis, liked to pretend he and Trey were friends. Well, Trey could call him Dan. Before he ripped out his throat.

Dan didn't have to be found. He had made it easy by contacting Trey. They were meeting in an out-of-the-way town, which put Trey on alert. Horton had said he needed to lay low, after his rather high-profile involvement in kidnapping and other irregularities. But Trey suspected Horton had other reasons for meeting like this. Because there was one thing Trey knew. Once you decided to kill someone, something had fundamentally changed in the relationship, and both parties often realized this.

Horton was far from stupid.

He'd arranged for them to meet in a coffee shop. It was dingy, the air conditioner working full blast in the summer's heat. The stale smells hit Trey hard, though he'd worked to make himself immune to sensory overload. Truth was, the higher the stakes, the more sensitive he became to all sensory information. Dealing in death was a high-stakes situation.

Horton sat in the corner, already drinking coffee, and Trey stopped to order his own cup, double double. As he pulled out a chair to sit opposite Horton, he considered his options. Best to be straightforward. Disarm Horton and force him at gunpoint into his car. Drive to somewhere deserted and let Horton out, allow him to run. Then shift and kill the man while wolf. The locals could count it as a wildlife kill. There wasn't a wolf population here so no innocent beast was likely to get blamed for the crime.

Horton took his time lifting his gaze to Trey's. The man saw too much unfortunately, and Trey felt wary, a prickling sensation across his shoulders. Something was up, that was clear. Trey wasn't the only one with plans.

Without preamble, Horton slid a piece of paper across the table. "Here's a picture, taken two weeks ago, printed today.

Turn it over."

Trey didn't want to. Horton's voice was too smug, too confident, and Trey seeing the picture was going to give Horton power over him. For the past few years, he'd worked to avoid allowing Horton any power over him.

"You should be in jail," Trey said quietly.

"Kingley thought otherwise."

Kingley should have let Horton take the fall while stepping back into the shadows, into the gray area where agents could operate without accountability. Why would Kingley have saved Horton? Because of his suspicions about Trey? Was Kingley using Horton to drag Trey back into the vortex that was domestic black ops? "What did Kingley pull you out for? Wetwork?"

Horton's eyes flashed with distaste. He didn't consider himself assassin material, even if he arranged people's deaths. "Look at the picture, Trey."

"Sure, Dan." Bracing himself, bracing his wolf because his sixth sense told him someone he protected was about to be threatened, Trey flipped the thin piece of paper over.

He didn't react. He didn't even process what he saw right away. After three and a half years, it was hard to believe he was looking at a picture of Jonah. Older, sharper, thinner. Far, far too thin. No longer raw-boned, Jonah was approaching skeletal.

Trey had wanted Jonah to be alive, yes, but not under Horton's power and not starving to death. What the fuck had happened?

It was hard to rip his gaze away, but Trey lifted his eyelashes to observe Horton. "Why are you showing me this photograph?"

Horton scratched his beard, his lip curling slightly. "I think you know."

"You think he's a wolf."

"I did," Horton acknowledged. "He's thin like one of those who can't eat enough, but I quickly realized my mistake. He's got the wrong temperament. There's no fight in him."

A sick feeling rose in Trey's chest, a battle with nausea and rage that he had to conquer for Jonah's sake. Clear thinking was essential.

"He was looking for you, Trey, as you've been looking for him."

Only Kingley could have possibly passed on that information, and Trey had been careful.

Horton's tone turned chiding. "Don't pretend you don't know him."

"He's changed." *Stick as close to the truth as possible.* "I knew him a few years ago, briefly."

"How?"

Trey gazed at Horton, unwilling to baldly state they had been lovers.

"Kingley thought you'd given up on men."

Trey shrugged. "Clearly I should have, if this is what happens to them. Why would you be interested in Jonah once you realized he wasn't a wolf?"

Here Horton let out a sigh. "I wasn't. I was *very* disappointed. Not only is he human, he's a bit touched and a bit dim. I didn't realize that was your style, Trey."

Trey didn't reveal his rage. Jonah was suffering and Horton understood fuck all about the lynx.

"He keeps asking to study university math." At Horton's guffaw, Trey wanted to reach across the table, clamp a hand on his throat and crush his windpipe.

But first he had to find out where Horton was keeping

Jonah. Trey asked the obvious question. "What are you going to do with him?"

"Blackmail you, of course. You appear to have some feelings of responsibility."

"If you intend to hold anything over me, you're going to have to reintroduce us. I know how this works. He could already be dead." His gaze flicked down to the picture. "He's not looking particularly healthy."

"We'll feed him better. And I don't mind a little introduction for a little cooperation."

"What kind of cooperation?"

"For starters, I'd like a liter of your blood. It doesn't have to be all at once."

Fury flowed through Trey. He knew what Horton was searching for—the werewolf gene. He wanted the blood sent for DNA analysis. Horton planned to engineer a secret Werewolf Genome Project and use it to control shapeshifters. Trey couldn't afford to hand him such power over himself and his family. Even his adult daughter, who wasn't a werewolf but a carrier, would be a target if this information was kept in Horton's secret hands.

Didn't matter right now. He still knew how to play this out. "First, I see Jonah, then the blood."

"That easily?" Horton sneered. "Please. What kind of fool do you think I am?"

Trey wanted to bare his teeth but couldn't afford to overreact to the taunt, so he quietly said, "I think you know I demand proof."

"Oh I can give you proof, no problem." Horton pushed away from the table and rose. "It's time for you to do as I say. If you don't, Jonah will die of thirst, a pretty painful way to expire. Slow too. No one knows where he is, you see." He looked down at Trey, watching him take in the information, trying to gauge how important Jonah was to Trey. "Therefore you will come with me."

And Trey obeyed, much as it galled him, leaving his car behind at the coffee shop. He climbed into the passenger seat of Horton's jeep and allowed Horton to take him God knows where. If he were purely rational, purely clinical, he would have attacked Horton anyway, killed him. He was a threat to a lot of people Trey cared about—his daughter, his niece and nephew. But Trey could not sacrifice Jonah, not without fighting his hardest to save him first.

Jonah had learned to wait. At least he figured that was the one accomplishment that kept him going. First he'd been in a holding pattern before Trey, grieving for his lost family, unsure how to move forward or if it was possible to move forward. Then Trey had arrived, stormed Jonah's defenses and left him naked in every way possible. No waiting during those three and half weeks that remained the most vivid days of his life. But afterwards, afterwards, there were endless months at home followed by a year and half searching and waiting—though at that point Jonah had lost track of what he was waiting for.

Then finally here, with Horton and the guard he occasionally sent in his place, bringing supplies so that Jonah could barely hang on. He knew he was weakening. Horton had asked him, his tone joking, if Jonah had wasting disease. Because he was getting thinner and thinner.

He wasn't shifting, and Jonah had thought it was a way for him to save on the calories. But somehow the cat, jailed within him, was draining Jonah's energy anyway. It didn't help that Horton was deliberately not feeding him enough either.

Jonah had considered his options and come to the decision that before he became too weak, he would have to kill Horton.

But not yet. Jonah felt he had a few weeks, maybe a couple of months, until he hit that point of no return.

If he did, he would die in here. Horton had made it clear that his death put the cell in complete lockdown. And no one was coming to the rescue.

Jonah could face death. He'd reached that point. Being a prisoner did that to a person, or at least to a lynx. But the lynx wanted to get that last kill in. Was straining for action. Perhaps it was good that it would be a few days before he saw Horton again.

Or that's what Jonah had thought before he observed Horton through the barred door, punching in the numbers that allowed him to enter.

He clanged the door shut and looked across at Jonah who made it a point not to challenge the man. His lynx found Jonah's way of stalking a little too slow and a little too stealthy, but was in fundamental agreement that their captor was being stalked. Jonah sometimes thought the reason his lynx stayed as quiescent as it did these days was because Horton was prey. There was a bloodthirsty side to him, hard to rouse, but strong once it had determined that an individual, be it Aaron or Horton, had to die.

It also interested Jonah that the longer his lynx stayed leashed within his human, the more of a split personality he felt. And it pleased Jonah that Horton didn't understand the first thing about him.

"You're an odd duck," said Horton. "I can't see what Trey ever saw in you, though maybe you were different a few years ago."

"Maybe," Jonah said vaguely.

Horton had brought a computer with him, which was a change of pace. Jonah found his interest picked up, and he wondered if this had the long-promised math texts on it.

Not that Jonah understood computers very well, so that would be a problem. But he understood that textbooks could be on computers.

"Math?" he asked, because his questions about math, while sincere, convinced Horton that Jonah was touched, not quite right, and completely not a threat.

The latter was important, that Horton didn't perceive Jonah to be a threat.

"No," said Horton briskly. "No math at all. Nevertheless I think it will be something that interests you."

Jonah eyed Horton then, realizing the man was acting differently today. There was an edge to his manner and speech, as if something important was happening. His lynx perked right up, looking for an opportunity to attack and Jonah had to get a grip on himself, keep control. He looked up into Horton's eyes, searching for clues as to what was going on.

Horton gave the slow smile he often delivered before a put-down, when he thought he was inflicting something however minor upon Jonah. But it was a question Horton asked. "Would you like to talk to Trey Walters?"

Jonah's body, weaker than he'd realized, seized and it became hard to breathe. His gaze widened as he stared at Horton, trying to see and smell truth.

Truth was there in the man, and Jonah gave it back to him.

"I want to talk to Trey, yes."

"First, I have to bind you to the bed."

Jonah paused, his cat protesting, yowling deep within him because he couldn't withstand another layer to this imprisonment.

Ultimately though, he had to talk to Trey. But he must

have been looking at Horton as if the man was prey, because Horton backed up and said warningly, "Understand this. If you don't do as I say, this conversation with Trey will not happen. Unless you know the passwords required and the protocol to get online with him."

Jonah considered. It might be possible to leap at Horton now, hurt and threaten him enough to put him through to Trey. Or he might still refuse. Or Jonah's cat might lose control and kill him anyway.

Jonah wanted to see Trey and alert him to the dangers Horton posed to shapeshifters. He'd waited a long time to do both things. They had become his purpose in life. He wasn't going to throw it away now.

So he went to the bed and allowed Horton to shackle him, when he hadn't been shackled since he'd awoken from his drugged state. He didn't allow his mind to dwell on the imprisoned wrist and ankle, but rather focused on the computer Horton now held on his lap as he keyed in different words and numbers.

Jonah couldn't rip his gaze away from that screen, even if it was angled away from him and difficult to see. His entire life was telescoping into this moment. His lynx was straining too. The combination of his prey being so close, of his body being bound, of his one chance to warn Trey before Jonah acted... His lynx was pushing to shift and it was the strangest sensation he'd ever experienced, as if the cat was just beneath his skin. Jonah's teeth seemed to sharpen, lengthen.

The presence of the cat so close to the surface should have been distracting, but given what Jonah wanted to accomplish, it wasn't.

The screen filled with Trey's face, and Jonah's throat squeezed tight. He couldn't speak in that moment.

"Dan, where is he?" Trey's voice, and it was a demand, not

a question. Trey was asking about Jonah, couldn't yet see Jonah given the way Horton held the screen.

"Patience," said Horton, though there was none of the smugness Jonah associated with him. Horton respected Trey, unlike Jonah. "He's here. As a precaution, he's been restrained for this interview. Normally, he's free to move around. He can tell you that himself."

Jonah couldn't see Trey all that clearly from this side view of the screen, but he heard Trey say, "Put him on."

The voice was different, whether due to the computer, due to the years that had passed, or due to the situation and Jonah's unstable body.

The reasons were irrelevant. Jonah had something to tell Trey and he needed to do it right. Time seemed to move slowly as Horton leaned towards Jonah and angled the computer up so the screen left Jonah face-to-face with Trey.

"Hello, Trey," said Jonah, and his words, betraying him, sounded eager.

Trey's only reaction was to blink, once. He was unable or unwilling to return the greeting.

There wasn't much time, and Jonah's lynx could smell Horton's blood now, flowing under the thin surface of his skin. Jonah's jaw seemed to move, lengthen, and his skin rippled with the power of the shift, fighting the shackles that held his human in place.

Words first. He realized Trey had already spoken his name once. "Jonah," he repeated, "are you all right?"

"Tell him you're fine," Horton said calmly as if Jonah were a simpleton who didn't know how to respond to such a question.

Trey winced then, surprising Jonah by breaking the mask he wore. His voice was low, the words anguished. "I am so sorry, Jonah."

The emotion behind the words shocked Jonah. After all this time, he'd trained himself to expect Trey not to care, to believe the caring had only ever been on Jonah's side. It might have been lopsided, but Trey was pained by Jonah's situation. And, he had to be warned. Jonah blurted, "Horton wants your blood."

Horton snatched the computer away and stepped out of range of Jonah. A mistake, his lynx seethed, fearing Jonah would not get another chance to attack.

He heard Trey demand, "Put Jonah back on, Dan."

"He's confused. I didn't make him that way either, though it doesn't matter if you believe me or not." Horton was pacing with the laptop now, his words coming out quick, unsettled that his plan was not going as he'd expected.

"I'll do fuck all if I don't see him again," Trey warned Horton.

"No. You're done. He's alive, as I promised, and I've given you proof."

"I said unharmed."

"I didn't harm him." Horton was leaving the room.

"Tell him I'm fine," Jonah called out, sounding rational, calm. He needed to reassure this new, uncertain Horton who clearly felt he was losing control of the situation.

His captor eyed Jonah, considering, while Trey again insisted he see Jonah, again warned Horton he wouldn't cooperate if he didn't. Directing his gaze back to the computer, Horton said, "There's nothing else to see, Trey, that's it. A more empty-headed young man, I have yet to meet."

"It'll go easier if you have my cooperation, Horton." There was an urgency to Trey's words and Jonah wondered at them. What did Trey want to see or say? Jonah might never know, because he was going to act, not wait.

Horton glanced over at Jonah, weighing his options. "I'm feeling generous. One minute left. That's it. I don't want to waste more time on this."

Once more, Horton walked over and Jonah's desire to see and talk to Trey again, even briefly, was stronger than he'd anticipated. He ruthlessly pushed it away, let his lynx pull forward, not trying to shift, because he would have blacked out, but putting lynx instincts ahead of all else.

Horton bent over and Jonah looked at his vulnerable neck, slightly protected by the way his head fell forward.

"Jonah," said Trey, and Jonah let his name wash over him, possibly for the last time. He didn't look at the screen though, too distracting, and Horton lifted his face to Jonah, impatience in his expression.

Never mind that his wrist held his body back, Jonah pounced, jerking his head forward. His teeth made contact, with skin, tendon, blood, and he bit into the soft tissue as deeply as he could.

They were his human teeth, yes, but sharper than a normal's and fueled by an anger that had been building during the months of his imprisonment.

Horton twisted, his scream strangled in his throat as Jonah pierced an artery. In this form he wasn't capable of crushing Horton's windpipe. But he had seized hold and he didn't let go as the blood began sliding down his throat. Horton fought back, kneeing him viciously in the groin. Pain swept through Jonah, almost cleansing, but he did not lessen his grip on his prey's neck. Horton's thumb found Jonah's eye, applied pressure, and Jonah steadfastly ignored the pain. His eye tore from the gouging, his vision went wonky, and blood started to wash down Jonah's cheek.

Jonah held on like he'd never let go.

It didn't take long before Horton's body weakened, but still Jonah didn't release him, instead waiting until all life drained away from the body before he finally relinquished Horton's throat. His dead prey slid to the floor.

Slowly, Jonah took in his surroundings. Everything had faded into the red of the fatal bite and he'd been aware of nothing but the killing of Horton.

He couldn't see out of one eye. It hurt like hell.

With his other eye, he saw the computer, his link to Trey on the floor, closed, presumably having fallen shut during their fight.

Now that his anger was fading, he tried to breathe through the agony in his eye and his groin, but the pain threatened to unman him. He lay down since he was shackled to the bed anyway, felt his chest rise and fall with effort, wondered if he would pass out.

The taste of blood in his mouth began to curdle. During the kill, it had been a kind of victory, even a release, for his prey to finally be caught, but now he recoiled against the killing in human form and had to work not to vomit.

The stench of death filled his nostrils—urine, feces, more blood. Jonah was going to die with these smells. His last memory.

No. He refused to go that way. If he couldn't escape his prison, he did not want to die shackled to this bed, beside Horton's body. So Jonah forced himself to rise again and leaned over at a painful angle, close enough to reach Horton. With his one free hand, he pulled the body closer and dug through pockets for the key to his shackles. He found it in Horton's pants.

It took a few minutes and some patience—something he was fast running out of—before he managed despite shaky hands to unlock his wrist and ankle.

He was on a downward slide from the adrenaline high of the kill, but he wasn't yet ready to collapse. Horton had told him Jonah couldn't get out through the barred doors without Horton's voice command. But Jonah tried repeating "exit" as Horton had done.

He pitched his voice lower and imitated Horton's tone and timbre—nothing happened.

He was losing his eye. His body was collapsing and the only thing Jonah could think to do was shift. The lynx was ready, even if his body was weak and weakening by the minute. Before he lost the ability completely, Jonah dropped to the floor and gave himself over to the shift that might not save him. But after months of human captivity he craved to be lynx this one last time.

Chapter Fifteen

Trey picked up the computer and slammed it against the wall. That was satisfying for all of one second. Then he heaved himself out of the chair and stalked across the room, flung open the door. Before the guard could react, Trey pulled the man's gun out of his holster and shot a bullet into the floor, an inch from the guard's foot.

"Dan Horton has been keeping a prisoner. I want you to take me to him."

The man's face went white, with anger more than panic. "Horton has been closemouthed about it."

"About *it*? So you know something."

"I don't know where the prisoner is being held."

Trey smelled truth and gripped the man by the throat. "Then tell me who does."

The man gazed back, silent.

"Horton is dead. I want that prisoner. You're going to figure out how I can get to him."

Under Trey's palm, the man swallowed. "Dead?" he rasped. "You're lying."

Trey shook his head and pulled back, still holding that gun. "Call him. Don't fuck around with me and call for help, because I'll shoot your hand before you're done."

The guard did, and to his credit his hands weren't shaking. Trey couldn't help hoping that Jonah would pick up the phone.

Jonah. God, Trey's chest felt like it was breaking into pieces, and he could barely breathe between the fury and fear generated by watching Jonah kill Horton. Trey was terrified he wouldn't be able to find Jonah and free him from his prison.

"No answer," said the guard.

"I want you to understand two things. One, I'm not interested in hurting you, but I will. Two, I want Horton's prisoner and I want him now." Trey had no problem talking as if he were interested in Jonah as a prisoner as long as he reached his goal—freeing the lynx. He wondered how the shifter had survived thus far. Werewolves couldn't endure being jailed.

"Leonard isn't a thinker, he does as he's told." The guard's brown eyes held something akin to shame, as if he was betraying a coworker.

"Phone him, put him on the line."

"He'll be sleeping."

"I don't care."

It took three rings to rouse the man and Leonard, presumably, said, "Hello?"

"I'm Trey Walters, Horton's colleague. I need you to come in immediately. I'll pick you up. Give me your address."

"Uh...okay." Leonard-who-does-as-he's-told obligingly gave his address, and Trey handed the phone back to the guard who stood in front of him.

"He's not stupid, just obedient. Few people have that number of his. He'll have assumed Horton gave it to you."

"Fine." This guard would simply have to deal with his own guilt later on. "If you've lied to me or led me astray, I'll let you know." Trey waited, in case the guard had something else to confess, but he just stared stonily back at Trey, anger banking there at having to hand Leonard over to him. "Horton was a complete asshole and deserves to be dead."

The man didn't disagree, but he didn't answer either.

"Let's hope we don't meet again," said Trey. "Give me the keys to your car."

The guard fished them out of his pocket and silently handed them over.

"Thank you." With that, Trey took off, driving ten minutes to pick up a not-terribly-awake Leonard and then, following Leonard's directions, another hour down a back road towards, apparently, Jonah. Trey avoided heavy-handed tactics with Leonard, instead implying that they were checking in on Horton who wasn't answering his phone. Leonard even checked on his own phone. It helped that Trey had impressive ID to flash *and* Horton had mentioned Trey to Leonard.

By the time they reached the field with the bunker—a fucking bunker for Christ's sake—Trey's wolf was straining within him. A sure sign that his emotions were out of control and the wolf wanted to take over, take care of the situation.

The wolf also wanted to rescue the lynx.

Trey turned off the ignition and turned to stare at Leonard who cleared his throat before saying, "Horton has told me this man might be dangerous. So I've always been careful."

"All right. Makes sense," he added leadingly, because he understood Leonard wanted to tell him something else.

"But he's never *appeared* dangerous," Leonard admitted, "only sickly. So I'm surprised."

Trey undid his seat belt and stepped out. "Let's see what's happened."

Leonard nodded, obviously steeling his nerve before he too exited the vehicle. *Careful*, Trey warned himself, *don't spook*

Leonard at the last moment. Because it was Leonard's retinal scan that would give access to this bunker. Hidden in a field, looking like a place out of World War II, Jonah was apparently stowed away in something that required the latest tech in order to gain entry.

Leonard made it most of the way to the first gate before he stopped, paused.

"Let's do it," said Trey, keeping all the impatience out of his voice, forcing a calm he didn't feel into his expression and his body stance. Leonard was convinced, and stepped up to the scanner. He waited ten seconds, keyed in the combination, and the lock clicked open.

They crossed into the bunker, shut the steel door behind them and Trey smelled blood, urine and...beneath those awful smells was lynx. Jonah. And he couldn't feel relief at having found Jonah, because the conditions were so godawful.

The cat snarled, loud enough for Leonard to hear. He looked to Trey, eyes going wide, and fear flowed off him. "What the fuck was that?"

"How do you open this second door?" Trey asked, voice steady. It was a door made of bars and the idea of Jonah behind them enraged him.

"Combination again," said Leonard, his voice shaky. "What the hell is happening?"

"Give it to me. The combination."

Leonard repeated five numbers and Trey punched them in, pushed a little to see the door give way and sit ajar. He kept a hand on that door and turned to his companion. "Leonard, go out and leave that steel door open. Get into the jeep and lock all the doors. Drive out of here and don't look back."

A soft hiss, barely audible, reached Trey's ears, and he didn't want Leonard to hear the lynx again, didn't want Leonard to see Jonah.

"Now," snapped Trey.

"But." Evidently Leonard was conflicted, and Trey wished he had psychic powers and could force Leonard to disappear from here, to forget everything that had happened today.

"This is my job, Leonard, to take care of this situation. It's *your* job to leave, to forget. You understand."

Leonard should. Horton often hinted at deep, dark secrets that his underlings weren't privy to. Leonard slowly said, "All right."

"Don't remember anything," Trey added for good measure.

With that, Leonard jerked a nod and fled. While the human wouldn't have Trey's sensitive nose, which was overwhelmed by the stench of death and blood, Leonard quite clearly had cottoned on to the fact someone had been killed. Thank God he didn't want to know more.

Trey waited for the motor to start, for the vehicle to drive away, before he stepped into the cell, into what had been Jonah's prison for fuck knows how long. Months? Years?

The first thing he saw was Horton's body. He'd bled out on the floor beside a bed, neck torn. No surprise there, given that before he'd lost the connection, he'd seen Jonah lunge for Horton's throat.

Where the hell was the lynx?

"Jonah?" he said quietly. No reply and Trey wondered if Jonah was so lost in his bloodlust he didn't recognize him. Being captive would wreak havoc with a shifter's sanity. Trey breathed in, smelled the lynx beneath the stench of death, and walked towards the dead body. He crouched down and came face to face with Jonah, green eyes glowing in the dim light under the bed.

Jonah spat-hissed, teeth bared, before he launched himself

from under the bed. It wasn't in Trey to defend himself, the guilt was that strong, though he stiffened in reaction to the lynx's movement.

Fur flashed by him as Jonah scrambled out the first door, the second door, and fled into the open field.

Fuck. Trey had been too focused on himself, too convinced Jonah had lost it and would attack him, when of course what he wanted was the freedom he'd been deprived of.

There was no point yelling. As he stripped off his clothing while striding outside, Trey pushed himself towards the shift. He fell as his wolf rose to the surface, desperate to turn wolf and chase down Jonah.

It had been three and a half years since he'd seen his mate, and he was not going to lose track of him now. Trey's world turned dark as he welcomed his wolf taking over.

The important thing was to move. He'd moved so little for so long that he needed to run. Without stopping, without thinking. There was a place he was aiming for like an arrow. He could feel it within him, but didn't think, just headed for home where he might be safe again.

He hadn't been safe for a very long time.

His body was weak, he acknowledged that, even as he refused to slow down. He pushed through the daylight and into the night. It had been months since he'd been out at night, and while he didn't have the time or energy to take in all the smells, sounds and sights, he nevertheless embraced everything about this night of freedom.

He didn't think it would last.

Something was chasing him. A predator. He too was a predator, and he had recently killed. But he was weak now and it was only within him to run, not stand and fight.

Night bled away as day invaded the sky, and still he ran, recognizing that it was almost over. He'd hoped to shake the predator, but he'd failed. His body was failing. He realized he hadn't been thinking clearly, that the first thing he'd required was food, especially after a shift. Instead he had rejected the body of his kill for reasons he did not want to consider, and he had not taken the time to hunt wild prey in these woods.

He worked to put as much distance as possible between himself and the cement room where he'd been held. Imprisoned. He didn't want to be near that prison when he died.

The predator was almost upon him, and Jonah stopped in a small field, whirled, and braced himself for the final attack.

A wolf barreled into the open where Jonah was taking a stand, and his world began to spin. He recognized this wolf, from long ago. He'd been stalked by this wolf before, then befriended.

Right now, the lynx didn't deal in friendship. He wanted to turn, run again, because it wasn't in him to attack or defend. But all his resources drained away and he couldn't move. He stayed rooted to the spot, his back arching, his fur standing straight up in display.

He wanted the wolf to *back off.*

At his second hiss, the wolf whined, which had Jonah's human asking questions he did not want asked. The wolf, *Trey,* of course he knew his name, whined and dropped to his belly, ears back. A submissive pose and Trey was not submissive, ever. Jonah couldn't process this. His body began to shake. He balked at the idea of collapsing though it was almost upon him. He stood there hissing as Trey inched closer and closer. And finally Jonah's body gave him no choice. His legs crumpled under the strain of the run, after months of captivity, and he fell to the ground.

At that Trey rose, of course he did, and Jonah warned him

away with a hiss. If he were human, he'd be saying, *Get the fuck away from me.*

Trey understood, because he didn't come closer. Instead he barked once, a command to stay put, Jonah's brain somehow dimly understood, before Trey disappeared.

The wolf had disappeared before, Jonah thought rather muzzily before he passed out.

Some time later he woke to the smell of fresh kill right in front of his nose, and he wasn't going to think about how vulnerable he was that Trey had returned and he hadn't been aware of it. His hunger roared awake and he tore into the flesh, gulping down what he needed till there was nothing left.

His body was still starving but now he could stand up again. He looked rather disdainfully at Trey and turned to stalk away.

The damned wolf followed him to the creek where he drank. Followed him as he continued on his way home. Brought him more food that Jonah could not resist eating. He was becoming increasingly aware that he'd never before been this thin, and he wondered how close to the line of starvation he'd been walking before Trey started feeding him.

And so the trek back home continued. A few times Trey tried to talk to him. He would shift to human but Jonah ignored him, except when there was food. His body couldn't resist fresh food. By the end of the journey, though, Jonah was hunting on his own and he thought then Trey would leave, since it seemed clear to both of them he was going to survive. Starvation had been avoided.

But no, the wolf insisted on shadowing him the entire time, catching up after Jonah's two attempts to elude him.

A week and a half later, Jonah reached home. There was no lifting of his heart, no joy. It was simply the end of a grueling trek. He wanted to be here, yes, but his weariness muted his reaction, and the most he felt was irritation with Trey who would not leave him alone in his exhaustion.

Ignoring the wolf, Jonah walked into the cave, placed his paw on the lever handle and shouldered his door open.

It had been years and little had changed. What surprised Jonah was the scent of Trey. Not immediate, but older, suggesting Trey had been here during Jonah's absence.

Something in Jonah softened at that. Trey had sought him out, had kept a promise—too late but still Jonah had not been entirely forgotten. It wouldn't fix the broken parts inside Jonah, but he felt less betrayed knowing Trey had eventually returned. Jonah prowled around the corners of the house, reacquainting himself, and finding Trey's smell in the food supplies and especially in the cot, where they'd shared each other.

Jonah didn't think he could forgive the wolf, no matter what had kept Trey away. But it felt better to know that Trey had made some effort.

Exhaustion pulled at Jonah and he crawled up into the cot. Yes, he was weak, because he breathed in Trey's scent, old and new, as he closed his eyes and simply slept.

Chapter Sixteen

Trey spent his days hunting, cooking and chopping wood. He took the time to go into town for food supplies, though he didn't like to be away from Jonah those few days. But winter was approaching and Trey wanted Jonah to have everything he would need for the season. Because Trey couldn't stay here indefinitely. He still had responsibilities to his extended family and felt obligated to check up on them.

Somehow in the past couple of years, after meeting Jonah, Trey was no longer estranged from his daughter, his nephew, his niece. He sometimes thought his meeting Jonah had cracked something open in him, allowing him to reconnect with these people who seemed to care for him, as he did them. Though not with the same strength of feeling he had for Jonah.

He didn't want to leave the lynx, but there was little point in saying that right now, because whenever he talked to Jonah there was no response, and sometimes, it appeared, no understanding. For Jonah stubbornly remained in cat form.

Or perhaps he needed to stay lynx. Perhaps he had been human too long. Trey had so much to ask him and Jonah apparently had so much he didn't want to answer—or no interest in doing so. Nevertheless Trey prepared for winter, in the hopes that Jonah would shift, regain his balance between his two forms. Trey's biggest fear was that the lynx would stay lynx forever, turn feral. He hoped this was not Jonah's real goal.

He didn't believe it could be since Jonah spent most of his day inside, sleeping and eating, recovering from what had happened to him.

The cat had been near skeletal. Close to death. Horton had been starving Jonah.

The thought made Trey's chest ache, as did Jonah's lying down so often and so still. As if he'd been through something from which he could not heal. And it had all happened because Jonah had met Trey.

One afternoon, Jonah stretched and made a rumble, not a purr, which Trey found himself listening for, but it *was* noise from the usually silent cat. Trey walked over and crouched beside him. He hadn't yet been allowed to touch Jonah and the desire to do so simply intensified with time.

Lynx-green eyes blinked at him.

"I wish you'd shift," Trey said in a low voice. He'd stated this before, more as a suggestion. But now he was pleading, because he didn't want to leave here until Jonah was human, and yet Trey had family responsibilities he could not ignore. "Please."

He'd told the lynx before about wanting to talk to him and Jonah had consistently looked away in apparent disinterest. At first Trey had the idea he'd show Jonah the letter he'd written that awful winter he'd come back to find this house empty, but the lynx clearly had no desire to see such a thing. Two days after their return Trey had crumpled the letter up and thrown it in the fire, unable to keep around a reminder of those feelings of sick loss that had accompanied the writing of those words.

At least Jonah was here now. At least Trey wasn't entirely alone. But old words would convince Jonah of nothing. What Trey had to do was say the right words now.

"I miss you." He could feel his face heat up, but it no longer mattered. His pride, always too strong in him and yet something that had kept him going when nothing else could, was being offered up to Jonah, and Jonah didn't care.

In fact, Jonah hissed in annoyance, as if Trey was an irritation he had to put up with.

"Jonah, are you punishing me?"

The lynx rose, his eyes filling with anger, which was perhaps an improvement over irritation and indifference.

"I think I deserve—"

The paw came at him with a speed that surprised Trey. Swiping through the air and whapping Trey across the face so his head turned to the side. It took him a moment to realize that the lynx's claws had been retracted and no blood had been drawn.

He hadn't been hit hard. It was a warning only.

"All right," Trey said slowly. "You're angry. Do you think you could be angry as a person, Jonah, because it would be a hell of a lot easier to shout this out than having me lecture you while you bat my face."

Jonah stalked out of the house, out of the cave, and loped away while Trey stood there, left behind, rubbing his jaw in frustration.

Trey feared for Jonah, locked into his lynx form only. While he didn't want to force himself on the lynx, Trey made the decision to touch Jonah. If he was suppressing his desire to shift, human contact might make a difference, might compel Jonah to turn.

Horton had laughed at Jonah's desire to study math, but Trey did not want Jonah to lose that. In fact he intended to bring back study materials. But the cat had to be human to take advantage of textbooks.

So when Jonah returned that evening, after dark, Trey fed

172

him without speaking. It was odd, what he was going to do. He'd never jumped a person like this, for these reasons, nor was he used to dealing in this kind of rejection. He didn't get attached to people, in general, and those he did, like his family, tended to want him around more than he wanted to be around. But Jonah was, as always, different.

He waited till Jonah was settled on the cot, his back curved as only a cat's could be, his body ready for sleep. Then Trey trod silently as he approached the lynx from behind. In one smooth movement, Trey threw himself onto the lynx, intent on capturing him.

Just before Trey landed, the cat tensed, half-turning as Trey's weight descended. Jonah yowled, twisting and struggling under Trey, and Trey fought to keep hold of him. He was strong, stronger than Jonah, but the cat had a flexibility and swiftness Trey did not possess.

The lynx scored a line down Trey's forearm but Trey refused to relinquish his grasp. There had been a theory behind this assault—the need for Jonah to return to his human form. But there was also a need within Trey, and wrong as this was, he found he couldn't let go, despite the pain and despite Jonah's anger. Cat muscles bunched beneath his grip, the fur sliding this way and that, and even with his experience in hand-to-hand fighting, Trey landed with his back on the wood floor, because he'd never before wrestled with a lynx who he didn't want to hurt.

Jonah pounced then, his sharp teeth taking Trey's open throat in his mouth.

The terrible thing was that a part of Trey didn't mind Jonah going through with it, ending it all. Trey was exhausted in his own way, not that he could speak of his weariness when Jonah had been through so much. And this stubborn fight with Jonah was sapping the last of his will.

The only thing he couldn't stand was the idea that Jonah would never recover from killing Trey. As that thought passed through Trey's mind, he realized the real danger was over, that if Jonah were going for the kill, Trey would be dying now. Instead heated breath blew across Trey's neck while sharp teeth did not actually break his skin.

A cat's warning. Again.

Trey's breath went in and out, shaky and loud, so unlike him and he couldn't stop it. He was shivering and it wasn't fear, it was longing. Though Jonah might hate him, might forever reject him, Jonah was also Trey's mate and Trey could not stifle his reaction.

Jonah released him then, pulled back enough to gaze, human awareness in those lynx eyes. Trey hadn't seen the lynx's expression appear so human in their time together, and he observed more than Trey might have wished Jonah to see, but he couldn't break the look away.

A soft noise escaped Jonah, and he leaned over to lick Trey's cheek, then his eyes, the too-rough tongue rasping like sandpaper over delicate skin. What the hell was Jonah doing?

He didn't dare ask, but allowed the contact, allowed Jonah to lick along his forearm that was bleeding freely from the scratch. The contact made Trey shiver again. He never shivered.

Jonah nosed Trey until he rose and lay down on the cot and pulled the sleeping bag around. He was too weary to plead again with Jonah to shift, and Jonah made no effort to leave him. Instead he lay on top of him, warming Trey who'd gotten too cold lying on the floor, and they both fell asleep, Trey deeply.

He hadn't slept so well for months.

Trey had accomplished what he'd intended, Jonah thought

rather grimly as he glanced down at his pale skinny body and reoriented himself to the human world, a world he'd had no interest in reentering until last night. But this morning, after Trey's full-body contact and their goddamned sleeping together—something that had been his cat's idea for fuck's sake—the urge to shift had become unbearable. Jonah had succumbed. The heat now rose off his skin and he breathed out a puff of air, visible in the cold morning.

It had been such a long time since he'd shifted in his own home, and everything about it felt utterly different. The invigoration that had always followed a shift was gone and Jonah was worn out. He had zero interest in sex. Age or experience had changed him, and he didn't know and didn't care why he wasn't aroused. He sure as hell didn't want to feel anything for Trey. Jonah reached for some clothing, somewhat musty after years of sitting in this cold, unused cave.

Then he stood, hands on hips, and gazed around. His sight was fully back. Slowly he reached up and touched the eye that Horton had gouged out before his death. It was whole, unharmed. Presumably Jonah had shifted in time to save it, not that he could remember that day clearly. It was all a blur, including his journey back here.

He was home. So familiar and yet...not. Something had altered and he guessed it was himself. He'd never figured that this house, this home, would be the best he could do with his life, but apparently it was so. At twenty-eight, he could accept that, if grudgingly. He'd accepted worse at the hands of Horton.

As he turned towards the doorway, he knew what he'd see—Trey, silent as a ghost, standing in the threshold, gaze hungry and haunted.

There was a time when Jonah would have cared, been moved by Trey's caring, by his *need*. But all Jonah felt was anger. Last night had been yet another small betrayal, because

Trey had known Jonah didn't want to be touched and he'd grabbed him anyway.

"Trey," he said quietly and nodded once.

Trey's gaze intensified but he didn't answer.

"I think I'd better eat."

As Trey stepped towards him, Jonah realized he was going to reach for him, and Jonah said, "No."

Trey froze while Jonah stepped around him and out of the room. He might have been able to sleep with Trey last night as a cat. His cat was ultimately more forgiving. His cat also thought it was his job to protect Trey, even protect Trey's feelings. But Jonah could not stand to be touched by anyone, including Trey.

He didn't want to think about Trey, wanted the man gone from his life. It was over. He'd discovered Trey was alive, not dead, he'd discovered that someone wanted to kill Trey and he'd stopped that, and he'd been freed. But that was an ending, not a fresh start between them. Jonah simply wanted to be alone. All those months in the cities searching, talking... It was over and he'd had enough.

"I'm sorry." Trey had followed him back to the main room and stood a good five feet away as Jonah rummaged through the food supplies—supplies built up by Trey—to make breakfast.

Jonah glanced up. "I don't want your apologies." He didn't and he had no desire to know what Trey was apologizing for.

"I couldn't get back here when I wanted to. I didn't mean to leave you waiting here for so long."

"Uh-huh." Of all things, Jonah had a hankering for porridge and jerky, a breakfast he had been sick of eating a couple of years ago.

"Okay, let's eat first," Trey said and went quiet, thankfully. Jonah liked silence. He was tired of noise. So they ate breakfast and washed up the dishes. Then Trey had to say, "I'd like to talk with you, Jonah."

"I'm pretty tired actually. It's been a while since I've shifted and it's worn me out."

"You're still recovering from almost starving to death."

Jonah set his jaw. He hadn't quite realized how thin he'd become. The weight loss had been so gradual and his state of mind so focused on just getting through the days. As he gained weight though, he could see that he'd been dangerously skinny. Right now, he was ready to rest, and he went to lie down on the cot Trey hadn't been using.

Trey plopped himself on his cot, knees too close, brushing near Jonah without quite touching, and Jonah edged away.

"My assignment was more complicated than I predicted," Trey continued.

Jonah looked up at the ceiling. "I really don't want to talk about this."

He hoped Trey would rise and leave, but he didn't move. Jonah thought if he closed his eyes he might be able to sleep.

"I came back here." There was a stubborn note in Trey's voice, almost embarrassed too, which despite himself Jonah found interesting. "It was almost but not quite two years later. You'd left."

"I know I left," snapped Jonah. The ceiling had rafters. He usually cleaned them once a year but now they were full of cobwebs. The entire place needed to be fixed up after years of neglect.

"Why did you leave?"

Jonah heaved a sigh. "It doesn't matter to you that I don't want to talk?"

"It matters." Trey reached for him, placed a hand on his

arm and Jonah jerked up to sitting, pulling away.

"Don't. Touch. Me." He looked at Trey then, saw his troubled expression. "I don't want you here. I don't want to talk to you. And I don't want you to touch me, hug me or *anything*. Are we clear on that?"

Trey's brow furrowed. "What was last night?"

"My lynx and I are not always in perfect agreement. You could say my lynx likes you better than I do."

"All right." Trey scrubbed his face.

"I left," said Jonah, "because I needed to know if you were alive or if you were dead. I got my answer. I'm back. And we're done."

"I understand you're angry—"

"You understand fuck all. Okay? *I* understand more than you do. You feel guilty. I'm sorry but I can't help you with that. You think I should understand you had to stay away, and I do. But it doesn't change how I feel about waiting for you for three and a half fucking years." Jonah swept a hand down between them. "It's over. I'm done. Whatever we had, it's broken. It meant a lot to me at one point, and now it doesn't. I honestly have no idea what it meant to you, but it no longer matters."

"It matters to me," Trey said in a low voice.

Jonah shrugged. "I can't help you with that."

"My boss, Kingley, was watching me too carefully. I couldn't afford to lead him back to you."

"Okay."

"But I should have. Better than you seeking me out and Horton finding you."

"It's done. I'm tired. I'd like to sleep."

"I'll have to leave in a few days."

Jonah lay down. He should have been happy to hear Trey

say that, since he wanted the man gone. But it reminded him of the first time Trey had left and how painful that had been.

"I need to check in on my family. Make sure they're okay."

Jonah slung an arm across his face. "How's the wife?"

"There is no wife, Jonah. I have a nephew, a niece."

"A brother, if I recall."

"That too." There was a long pause. "I have a daughter."

Jonah didn't want to hear more about Trey's family. He didn't.

"She's your age."

"*My* age?" Jonah let his arm fall, doing the math. Trey had been a teenaged dad—barely. Well what do you know, being indifferent to Trey brought out all sorts of confidences. Trey would never have told him anything if Jonah had actually been asking questions, shown curiosity, been invested in this conversation. Christ.

"I didn't know about my daughter for her first fifteen years."

"Oh yeah. You had a lot of sex at too young an age."

Trey grunted. "I'll come back."

"Don't bother saying that."

"Look—"

"I don't want to hear it, Trey."

Trey's face darkened. "I'll be back."

I'd rather you didn't. But the words, dammit, stuck in Jonah's throat and he couldn't push them out. Fine, let it be an experiment. See how long it took this time. "See you in three years then."

Shaking his head, Trey clenched a fist. "You've got enough food and firewood for quite a while."

"Thank you for that." Jonah closed his eyes, turned on his side, back to Trey. "I really am quite tired."

He expected Trey to talk more, argue more, but the wolf remained silent, still. And in that stillness, Jonah fell asleep.

Chapter Seventeen

It was a relief when Trey left. It was, and yet it galled Jonah that he missed Trey's presence. He was too angry, too hollowed out, to miss anyone or anything. He wanted his place to himself, he wanted his life back. He'd never been the happiest person in the world, but at least he'd had his own way of living on his terms. The past two years had robbed him of something.

Mostly he tried not to think about what had happened. In some ways, by going through the motions of his day, he slipped back in time. Okay, he slept more than he used to, still recovering, but otherwise the familiarity soothed him, when it used to drive him mad with boredom and loneliness.

A month passed in this way—too early for Jonah to think that Trey was proving him right by not returning this time. He actually did expect Trey to come back, but in the far-distant future, in years. Trey after all was an important man with important things to do and Jonah...wasn't.

But he had killed for Trey, whether or not Trey understood it as such, and Jonah felt the same way about Horton's murder as he did about Aaron's. A long time ago, Jonah had silently vowed he would keep Trey safe and he had held true to that. Despite the way things had ended between them, that fact gave Jonah intense satisfaction.

The first blizzard arrived. He spent some time as lynx, some as human, enjoying the snow that had not been his to enjoy in the city. Knowing he could shift back and forth between his two forms also soothed and healed him, made him feel less like a split personality and more whole. Still empty but not quite as broken.

He was sleeping in his cot in the dead of night when someone tromped into the cave. Jonah surged awake, heart racing, as Trey's voice reached him through the door.

"It's me."

Jonah could only blink in astonishment and watch while Trey pushed on through, flashlight in hand, clad in winter gear, carrying a backpack of all things.

He'd expected Trey to return as a wolf. He picked up his lamp on the floor and turned it on, holding it aloft.

"What are you doing here?" Jonah demanded and the barely there smile on Trey's lips disappeared.

"I told you I'd come back."

"In the middle of the night? As *human*?"

Trey eyed Jonah, as if trying to understand his point. Jonah was trying to understand it too, to be honest. "I can carry things in as human. That's how we get food supplies here."

We. Jonah's lip curled at the word.

"I'm sorry I woke you."

"What were you doing?"

Trey let his backpack drop to the ground. "When?"

"What did you spend a month and a half doing?"

Trey's mouth thinned and his tone turned flat, brittle. Jonah didn't recall Trey being brittle. "I helped rescue a boy from my brother. I killed two werewolves, but I didn't manage to kill my brother."

His brother, the unstable killer. The mere mention of Gabriel's name had always wounded Trey. Suddenly Jonah no longer wanted to argue with Trey, and brother-killing was a topic he had no desire to explore. "Is the boy all right?"

"He will be. He's with *his* brother, who is responsible and sane."

"I'm glad."

"Don't get out of bed, it's too cold," Trey said quickly.

Jonah nevertheless went to the back room and got Trey some bedding, returned to throw it on Trey's cot and dived into his warm sleeping bag.

"Thank you, Jonah."

"I'm going back to sleep." He didn't actually know if he would, but his anger had morphed into something like confusion, simply because of this boy Trey had rescued. Jonah had been inwardly sneering at Trey's self-importance and how Trey used it as an excuse for letting Jonah down. But Trey had helped a young boy, rescued him, and it had been painful for Trey because Gabriel was involved.

The idea that he was somehow softening in his feelings for Trey was too unsettling to contemplate. Jonah didn't want to admire Trey. Admiration led to other feelings and he couldn't afford to depend on Trey again, in any way. No matter how worthy Trey's deeds or how important his actions.

Once Trey was settled in his own cot, he announced, "I'm glad to be back," in a voice that sounded entirely satisfied at having returned. As though coming here gave Trey a sense of coming home. Was that possible?

It gave Jonah pause, that his grudging acceptance of Trey's presence should make Trey feel welcome. He would have thought Trey had others who appreciated him more. Who welcomed him home instead of demanding to know why he'd come back. Who greeted him with a smile instead of wiping the smile off Trey's face.

Surely Trey had more than Jonah in this world.

"Jonah?"

"What?" he replied, alarmed by how disconcerted he felt.

"You been okay?"

What was that supposed to mean? *Probably* didn't seem like the right answer. "Sure." He tried to mean it. It wasn't too far off the mark.

"Good. I hated coming here after you disappeared and I didn't know where you were. It feels"—Trey huffed out a breath Jonah could hear in the dark—"right that you're here."

Jonah rolled his eyes, in vain, because he was moved by Trey's statement when he didn't want to be. In response he pretended he'd fallen back to sleep. Not that Trey would be fooled, but he lapsed into silence too. They both lay awake for quite a while. Jonah wondered if he'd stay awake all night long, but at some point he dropped off into a dream.

In the dream, he was different, his old self, and he yearned for contact, as he had all those years ago. This time he was alone but not alone. He kept reaching for Trey, again and again. Despite the fact Jonah stood right beside Trey, he couldn't actually touch him. Each time he tried, everything turned to mist. Dissolved. Until Trey gave up and went away.

At least Jonah had gained some weight. Not enough, but nevertheless a step in the right direction. And maybe it was wishful thinking more than real observation, but Jonah seemed less jumpy and angry than he'd been when Trey had left a month and a half ago. The lynx might have needed some time to himself.

The idea that Jonah did better without Trey around did not

sit well. Because Trey wanted to be with Jonah all the time. It figured. Trey had spent decades cultivating his lone-wolf lifestyle and it had come to this—feeling that Jonah was his mate and wanting to be with him.

Trey could imagine how well such a declaration to Jonah would go down. With Jonah's current mood, his reaction would be along the lines of snarling, *What the fuck are you talking about?*

So he decided to keep to more mundane topics of conversation.

"Sleep well?" he asked a tousled Jonah who sat up on his cot.

"Sure." Jonah didn't really want to be talking to him since his return. Most mornings, silence lay between them. But for whatever reason, today Trey couldn't keep quiet. Maybe it was the sunshine lighting up the usually dim house, that moment in the morning when the angle of the sun's rays struck the skylight just right.

And there it came, for the first time since they'd been reunited, a faint whiff of arousal—Jonah's. Unlike four years ago when Jonah hadn't realized Trey could scent his attraction, this time Jonah did and that realization promptly doused the spark that had flared. Jonah's eyes narrowed and despite his reddening face, he said flatly, "Forget it."

Trey stared while Jonah sheered his gaze away, pulled on his winter gear and went outside. He was back in a few minutes, so he hadn't decided to go for a long walk, just take a leak. And by the time Jonah sat by the fire to eat the breakfast Trey had made, the arousal or at least what Trey could sense of it, was completely gone. He supposed the attraction had snuck up on Jonah unawares, as he was waking. Still it was reassuring to know something lingered from their affair. It gave Trey hope.

"How are the textbooks?" Trey had been dead set on bringing Jonah something he would value, and his reward had been watching a rapt Jonah pore through the texts.

"Thank you for buying them for me." A careful expression of appreciation, but not what Trey wanted.

"I'm not asking for a thank-you. I'm asking how you find them. If they're at the right level for you."

"The algebra is too easy. The calculus is good." Suspicion lit Jonah's eyes for reasons beyond Trey's understanding. "Why?"

"I'll bring second-year algebra next time."

"When are you leaving?" The question was pitched to be casual, but didn't quite hit the mark. Unfortunately Trey was unable to tell if Jonah looked forward to his departure or resented it. Maybe it was both.

"No immediate plans. I'll check in with them in a month."

"A *month*?"

Trey turned to face Jonah who was closer than he usually got. His gaze apparently unnerved the lynx, because he shrank back.

Shit. Maybe not less jumpy. Trey faced the fire and sighed. "I spent a month with you last time."

"That's true. Each visit is a month long. I should have realized that."

He didn't want to leave at all. Trey simply wanted to stay. He was tired of being responsible for others, he was tired of *killing* others, no matter how deranged or violent these individuals had become. Too old for the job, he supposed. Something in him was weakening. There was no future in the job, only bleakness.

He grimly held on to the hope that another month together with Jonah would build some trust between them, build a future, now that Jonah was stronger physically, now that Jonah was human for at least half the time.

But he couldn't share these thoughts. Jonah wouldn't appreciate it. Trey stuck with a simple statement. "I'd rather stay longer than a month."

"I'm sure."

"Jonah."

He stood, waved a hand between them. "Sorry. Don't mind me."

"I do mind you. I think about you all the time."

"Don't. You should really leave, you know?"

Trey wanted to point out that Jonah hadn't told him to, hadn't insisted he go, but he wasn't ready to bring that to a head. "His name was Ira."

"Huh?"

"The boy I helped rescue. Ira. Seven years old. Very cute kid." Trey knew Jonah had been affected by the story, perhaps because of the brothers angle.

"I'm glad he's safe now."

"Pretty much. My brother has disappeared. Ira won't be so safe if Gabriel comes back. That's why I like to check in."

Jonah sat down again, slanting a hard look at Trey. "Bring your brother here. I'll kill him."

Never. "He's strong and he's vicious. I wouldn't chance it."

"Once I decide I'm going to kill someone, I do it." Jonah's mouth quirked. "As you've observed."

Trey nodded, treading carefully, because until now Jonah had refused to speak of any of this. "Horton?"

As he fiddled with his spoon, Jonah's eyes brightened with something like hate, then he jerked the spoon back and forth between them. "He claimed he was going to tell me about you, where you were. Instead he drugged me, believing I was a werewolf. When he realized I wasn't, he told me he wanted your blood. At which point I decided to kill him. But I wanted to see you first, warn you."

Trey was finding it hard to breathe. "You waited for me."

His eyes were vivid, alive, angry. "I waited too long for you, in different places and for different reasons. But yes, I waited in that prison for you."

"How long were you there?"

"Months. I weakened, lost track of time. I don't usually do that."

"He was starving you to death." *Because of me.* The guilt was hard to bear, but Trey would bulldoze his way through it, churning stomach or no.

Jonah shrugged, then glanced at Trey again, looking for a reaction. "Horton wasn't my first kill, Aaron was."

"Aaron Smythe, your mother's ex?" Trey asked and watched Jonah nod. "He used to hit you."

Jonah laughed, little humor in it. "He put my mother in a coma. She died. I stalked and killed him. Ripped out his throat. It's more satisfying to rip out a person's throat when you're lynx. But I had fewer choices with Horton."

"Jonah—" He knew it was too soon, but his body insisted on reaching for him, insisted that what Jonah needed was the contact.

"No." Jonah was already standing, backing up to the cot, before Trey's hand had gotten near him.

"What happened there?" demanded Trey. "Why are you like this?"

Jonah frowned. "I am telling you what happened."

You won't let me touch you. But Trey bit down, didn't speak.

Those words weren't going to help here and now.

Somehow Jonah understood. "I spent a *lot* of time as human. I discovered I don't like to be touched by people. I don't like it all. No one assaulted me, well, apart from Aaron and Horton, but they're dead."

"What did Horton do?"

"He shackled me, Trey. You saw it. He would put those restraints on me, twice, and it made my skin crawl." The expression of revulsion on Jonah's face scared Trey, scared him for Jonah's sake.

"I'm not them. You know that."

"Sure. I know that. But I was waiting for you. I spent too much time thinking about you, and it's a mess in my head. You're all tied up with Horton." There was the faintest trace of an apology in Jonah's expression. "So don't touch me."

Trey could feel his face fall, didn't know what to say. "I'm so sorry," he said hoarsely. "I never wanted this for you. I was trying to protect you from exactly this."

"I'm glad you protected Ira, Trey, I am. I think that you're a good person. But..." Jonah gestured, a flip of one hand that was part shrug, part goodbye. "You want something from me I cannot give."

"I want to be with you, and that's enough. You're giving me that."

"Not what I mean. I don't want to have sex with you."

"I got that message. Really. But being in the same room with you, living with you—I want those things too."

Jonah looked frankly puzzled. "You do?"

Of all things, Trey felt himself smile. Because he'd surprised his lover who was not at this moment his lover. And because it was true. "Of course I do."

Chapter Eighteen

One week after Trey departed for the second time that winter, he clomped back into the house in the middle of the afternoon. Here Jonah had been gearing himself up for a long haul, telling himself not to expect Trey back till spring or summer, if that, and Trey was standing in front of him, literally steaming.

"Overdressed?" Jonah ventured once he managed to stop staring.

Trey threw him a quick smile. His smiles were rare, mostly because Jonah didn't want them to work their charm on him, and Trey didn't smile without some encouragement. Usually. "It's pretty mild out for February."

He stripped off the winter gear until he stood in long underwear and Jonah had to work at not observing the powerful body beneath the thin material. Trey was forty-four now, his birthday had been in January—not that they'd celebrated—and he was the fittest man Jonah had ever met.

Dammit, he felt shy and awkward, and he didn't want to feel that way, for all kinds of reasons.

"Brought you some more textbooks." Trey actually sounded excited. It was something, for Trey to be excited on Jonah's behalf, and he found himself wondering again why Trey tried so hard for him. Anyone else would have been long gone.

Trey *would* be gone, Jonah reminded himself. He had people to protect. "How's Ira?"

"He's good, apparently. I didn't go see them. I just phoned, talked to everyone, including a couple of wolves who've been scouting out areas for me. I also bought a satellite phone and went to a university bookstore."

Jonah got stuck on *university bookstore*. Trey had gone there for him.

"Takes that long to get in and out when you're walking," Trey pointed out, as if Jonah were doubting him in some way.

"Yes."

"So." Trey gestured towards the books he'd placed on Jonah's cot. "Going to take a look?"

Gawd, this bashfulness was pathetic and annoying, and a week's absence and proffered textbooks the cause of it. Jonah grabbed for a book, hoping its content would distract him enough not to feel so... Well, just not to feel.

He'd missed Trey. That was the problem.

Big problem. If he began to depend on Trey again, he wasn't sure he could deal with never knowing when Trey would be here, and when he'd be gone for years. Jonah didn't have much in the way of resources. There wasn't exactly anyone else he could depend on. Just things—house, food, books.

He looked down and picked up the gift to run his hands over the cover and the spine. Opening the text, he pressed his face against the pages, breathing in the awful yet special new-book smell. Until Trey had started bringing these presents, Jonah had only had musty old-book smells to enjoy. He'd never been able to afford to spend money on extras when his food-supply money was limited and his income zilch.

He flipped to the beginning, reading the title page, copyright page, dedication. Without taking his gaze off the book, he said, "Thank you."

"I want you to be happy."

Last month, Jonah would have sneered or rolled his eyes or something to belittle such a statement. Today the words made him feel warm inside and his face heated up a little. Trey was standing close, close enough to lay a hand on Jonah's shoulder. The idea made him twitchy and yet...it wasn't entirely unappealing.

That was a first.

He turned the page, deciding to look at the book and no longer think about Trey.

"I'm going to wash, if that's okay. I'm drenched in sweat." Trey's gaze was upon him and Jonah made it a point not to look up.

"Sure."

"Is it too easy again?"

"Huh?" Nothing seemed easy right now.

"The text. Is it too easy, like the other two?"

Oh. "Well, I don't know, I've barely looked at it." Jonah glanced up in exasperation, only to find Trey completely stripped down. "You haven't gotten the water yet."

Trey grinned. "Don't worry."

Jonah stared, baffled by Trey's good mood. Then watched as he picked up the two pails used for this purpose and dashed out, buck naked, to fill them with snow.

Returning in less than two minutes, he said, "See? I didn't freeze."

But he gathered back by the fire, poked it, fed it, and Jonah had to rip his gaze away from the curve of Trey's buttocks, the slope of his shoulder. He'd forgotten how beautiful he found Trey's body to be. Or maybe forgotten was the wrong word, because earlier he had seen Trey naked and had felt next to nothing.

Something was waking up inside him, and while the idea of loving Trey again filled him with dread, he couldn't entirely regret the rebirth of these feelings, and the lifting of the deadening emotion that he'd carried with him for months and months.

"So?" Trey jerked his head towards Jonah. "Why aren't you reading?"

Jonah stared, feeling a little doomed, and Trey's expression shifted from inquiring to solemn, mirroring Jonah's own.

"I know it will be okay, Jonah."

He could have played dumb but it wasn't in him. "I don't know that."

Trey looked torn and Jonah could guess he was debating with himself whether to approach Jonah or not.

Not. At least *not yet.* Jonah returned to the book, flipped the page, began reading. Determined to think about anything but Trey, and Trey went back to washing. Jonah relaxed at that and it didn't actually take long to become engrossed in the math.

However, the awareness didn't leave him over the next few days. It reminded him of that first time he'd met Trey and had gradually become aware of the wolf's body, the way he moved, the way he smelled. Jonah had been convinced he'd never be drawn to Trey again. He had miscalculated entirely. Yes, he was angry that months had turned into four years, that part of his time of waiting and thinking endlessly about Trey had been spent in Horton's cell.

But it had become difficult to continue to hate Trey for it. Not when he kept coming back offering gifts, not when he went out to make sure his kin, including seven-year-old boys, were safe.

Not when he was here.

That counted for more than Jonah had ever realized. For clearly the anger was draining away the longer Trey stayed with him.

One evening Trey sat on his cot, bent over some book he'd brought with him. A mystery. He liked to read fiction Jonah had come to learn. He stared at the broad back, thought about leaning against it. Problem was that Trey would then turn around to hold and overwhelm him, and Jonah didn't actually want that, wasn't ready for it.

He just wanted to lean against that back.

Trey didn't touch him when Jonah didn't want him to, not since he'd leapt on Jonah's lynx to force Jonah to shift to human. So why did it seem like this huge thing, to slide off his cot and sit on Trey's?

He'd intended to return to his book but couldn't look away from his erstwhile lover.

Well, he would rise and if Trey looked backward, he'd go get a glass of water.

But Trey didn't glance around. He got like this sometimes when he was reading, oblivious to Jonah and the world surrounding him.

Before he could think on it further, Jonah tucked a leg under himself and plopped down directly behind Trey, so they were mere inches apart. While Trey didn't move at all, a kind of tension suddenly held his body in position, and Jonah suspected he was no longer reading his book.

Tentatively, it had been so long, Jonah placed his forehead between Trey's shoulder blades and breathed in Trey's scent.

His back was warm and strong, and Jonah lifted his forearms to rest on Trey's shoulders as he turned his face to lean a cheek against Trey's spine.

"Trey," Jonah murmured.

"Hmmm?"

"Don't turn around, okay?"

"All right."

It was intoxicating, in the oddest way. Jonah had a semi, but he wasn't strongly aroused. He felt...relaxed, in a way he hadn't for the longest time. A wave of relief passed through him and he remembered how it had been before when they were together, the sense of coming home that Trey had given him. Might be able to give again, even if Jonah couldn't enter into intimacy with the same kind of naivety he'd had at twenty-four years of age.

He found he wanted to speak. "I wish I hadn't become like this. I wish it was back to when we first met."

"Jonah," said Trey in a low voice, a kind of warning, a kind of plea.

"But I'm not like that now."

"Not now. You waited too long for me. It's my turn to wait for you."

"Is that what you're doing?" Jonah smiled against Trey's back, until the next thought struck him. "For how long?"

Trey's back rippled with his shrug. "For however long it takes, since you're my mate." The last word was said with some intensity.

"I'm your mate?" Jonah had never heard Trey use that term before. "What does that mean?"

"It means we should be together."

"I don't want to have sex with you." Not entirely true, but not entirely untrue either.

"Yet we're still together. It's enough." *For now* was implied.

"The cities," said Jonah, apropos of nothing, "were fascinating and repugnant. I couldn't stay away and yet the idea of going back to them is awful to me."

"Then we won't go to cities."

Leaning against Trey like this made Jonah feel strangely sleepy, strangely soothed. He didn't feel like editing his thoughts. "By and large, the people in the city actually treated me quite well. They wanted me to be warm and fed, they wanted me to be able to support myself. They would touch me occasionally. A hug, a pat, or something else. Not too much but I disliked it."

"How many people did you sleep with?"

"How many?" Jonah was close to snickering, which was juvenile, but he sensed jealousy here and he kind of liked it. "Let me think."

"*Jonah.* I'm worried about you."

"Oh, you think I had a bad experience? No, I couldn't bear the thought of sleeping with someone else. It..." It had freaked him out. And as the months passed by, he'd developed this aversion to touch. But here he was leaning against Trey's solid back and it felt good, right.

"Some shifters get messed up when they stay too long in their human form." Trey was speaking carefully now. "I think that's been part of your aversion. You need the balance of human and cat, otherwise things get out of whack. You won't feel comfortable in your skin, let alone others touching your skin."

"But I would leave the city, go to the country and be lynx."

"How often?"

"Every couple of months."

"And how often do you shift now?"

"Every couple of days," he admitted. "A week at most."

"We won't go to cities," Trey repeated.

"What about you, when you're human for a long time?"

"Well, it makes me tense."

Jonah breathed in through his nose. "You don't seem tense now."

"I'm not," Trey said softly.

But Trey was aroused while Jonah was sleepy, relaxed. He wanted to end it while things felt so good between them. Comfortable. He hadn't been comfortable with someone for ages. So he backed up, slipped over to his own cot, and only then did Trey turn. His eyes were slumberous, sexy, warm. All those things.

"I'm tired," said Jonah quickly.

"I know." Trey wasn't offended. In fact, he looked...lighter than he had in ages. Perhaps Jonah's contact had accomplished that. Trey's mouth kicked up. "You can lean against me any time you want."

The stupidest question came out of Jonah's mouth. He had sworn not to ask and yet the words escaped. "When are you leaving next?"

"I'll do the same thing in a month. I expect they'll be fine and I'll be back. If there's a problem, I'll be gone longer. Not entirely predictable, I'm afraid. I can't promise quick returns." There was a certain anxiety there, beneath the surface of Trey's expression, a worry about how Jonah would take this information.

Jonah nodded. "Okay."

Truth was, it might be okay, or Trey might disappear for ages. But tonight wasn't the night to dwell on that. Instead Jonah lay down and thought about the musculature of Trey's powerful back, shaped by spine and shoulder blades. He'd breathed in the tang of Trey's wolf, his musky deep scent.

Horton had wanted Trey's blood and he hadn't got it. Throughout the ordeal and the aftermath, that was something Jonah remained proud of. He was almost dozing before he realized Trey had crouched beside his cot, close but not too close.

"Jonah."

He lifted eyelashes to look at that now-familiar face. "Yeah?"

"I love you." The delivery wasn't fervent or passionate. It was a statement of fact, and Jonah didn't know what to do with it.

So he said, "Okay."

Before he had time to wonder if he'd answered wrong, Trey smiled and rose, walked away.

Chapter Nineteen

The next morning Jonah chose not to deal with the can of worms he'd opened by leaning against Trey's back. Instead he shifted to lynx and ventured out into sunshine and snow for the day, continuing his long reacquaintance with the area he considered home. With the mild temperatures, deer were plentiful this winter. There was plenty of potential firewood—not that they needed any since Trey had been hard at work providing for them.

But his sojourn proved not entirely successful. After he came back inside, still lynx, the first thing Jonah found himself doing was going up to Trey and rubbing against him, purring. He then lay by the fire as Trey cooked food. He could practically smell Trey's happiness, and there was a recognition of the power he held over Trey if Jonah's actions mattered this much.

Yes, Trey had been wrong to leave Jonah for years, but it clearly wasn't from not caring. Jonah was coming to accept that, accept that Trey would leave him again too. Maybe next time it was for the long haul, Jonah would be mature enough to handle it. He'd been young, not only in years, he recognized. Strangely sheltered and unused to the feelings he'd developed so suddenly, almost brutally, for Trey, Jonah hadn't been able to cope with the fallout.

Next time he vowed to handle himself differently. He knew what making such a vow to himself meant—that he and Trey were about to become lovers again. Jonah was ready. Almost. He stayed lynx for another day, preparing himself for what was to come.

When Jonah rose, shook himself and stalked into the back room, Trey had a good idea why he'd done so. He waited. It seemed to him that their relationship had developed around the concept of waiting. Jonah had done more than his share, Trey was quick to recognize. But still, he hoped that one day in the not too distant future, their relationship could be about more than waiting and its attendant problems.

Trey glanced around, working hard not to think about what Jonah was doing or in what state of mind he'd be once he emerged from the shift. This house was wonderful in its way, but also oppressively small. Trey would like for them to be able to settle elsewhere, especially for the winter, and perhaps only spend part of the summer here.

Jonah should get his university degree and the logistics of doing such a thing, even online, were difficult. While Trey could make his satellite phone receive rerouted phone calls out here— something he'd set up during his last journey into town—that wasn't enough to run a computer on.

They could live in the country, not in town, but somewhere with electricity and other amenities—unlike here.

If only Trey didn't continue to fear that Kingley would discover Jonah. Kingley remained rather fixated on Trey and werewolves, despite him having quit everything to do with all agencies. Despite Kingley not being able to find Trey at the moment.

No doubt Horton's bloody death had something to do with Kingley's interest. He believed a wolf in human form had killed Horton.

Trey shook his head. This wasn't where he wanted his thoughts to go. He'd been happy lately, believing there was a future for him and Jonah. That belief was hard to trust and yet he could not turn away from it. Not when Jonah, too, seemed to be more himself, instead of the angry, skittish lynx he'd first returned with.

From the other night, Trey could still feel Jonah pressed against his back, arms across his shoulders. He wanted that again, and more. As Trey finished washing up the last of the dishes, he heard Jonah getting dressed.

He was drying his hands as Jonah stepped past the threshold and into the main room. Trey wasn't much given to feeling awkward. He'd had to get rid of that early on to survive, but he couldn't exactly go stony-faced now. Instead he wiped his already dry hands, the cloth feeling oddly rough on suddenly sensitized skin. A light shiver ran across his shoulders.

He made himself look at Jonah, because it didn't matter if Trey could scent arousal if Jonah wasn't ready.

The expression on Jonah's face wasn't reluctance, more that of one who'd given up fighting something, given in.

Trey put the cloth down. "Come here."

As soon as the words were out of his mouth, he wished he could take them back because Jonah had stiffened.

"Jonah—"

"Shhh." With a faint smile, Jonah shook his head and walked forward. Trey stood stock-still. It wasn't until Jonah lifted his arms to embrace Trey that he reciprocated, pulling Jonah hard against him, burying his face in Jonah's neck.

Careful, careful, he thought, worried he was holding Jonah too tight. But Jonah's arms were banded around him too.

Trey shuddered. He hadn't meant to, didn't mean to be

breathing so harshly either. But the longing rose hard within him. He tried to be aware of Jonah retreating, pulling back, so that Trey wouldn't be holding him when he didn't want to be held. That was important.

Of all things, Jonah laughed. It was short, and Jonah still hadn't lessened his hold on Trey, but its meaning was beyond him. This Jonah had become much more complex than the Jonah he first knew.

"Trey?" He spoke into Trey's shoulder.

Trey grunted, an approximation to speech.

"I feel so relieved."

"Relieved?" At this Trey did pull back, searching Jonah's face which showed...pleasure.

"Yeah, I thought I wouldn't feel good in your arms again. I thought..." Jonah lifted one shoulder, "...it was over for us. I really did. I'm glad I was wrong."

At that point Trey became aware—though how could he not have been aware before?—that they both were hard.

Jonah pushed against him, his eyes widening in suggestion. "So, what are we going to do?"

Trey slid his palm down Jonah's long back, up again. "We don't have to do anything."

Jonah's mouth curved. "Always so noble. But, this time, I think we do."

He took Trey's hands and backed up, leading them towards a cot. Because Trey was hesitant to do anything, Jonah took the initiative, sliding hands under Trey's sweater and shirt, pulling off his clothes, then stripping himself so they were naked with each other.

Despite Trey's shivering and the time that had passed since they'd last been naked together, it was the most natural thing in the world. They didn't kiss till almost near the end, when Jonah put his large hand around the back of Trey's head and angled his mouth down.

"Come here," he murmured, saying Trey's words back to him as he smiled. Trey came as their mouths met, lips together then tongues tangling as Jonah pumped his too-sensitive cock with his strong, warm palm.

He barely had time to begin to worry about Jonah when his lover joined him, come slicking Trey's hand and Jonah's cock, while he groaned under Trey's mouth and in his arms.

They collapsed on the cot, Trey under Jonah, who was laughing again.

With his dry hand, Trey cupped his cheek. "Okay?"

Jonah's eyes were bright. "I didn't think it would be so easy."

"*Easy?*" repeated Trey in disbelief. These past few months had been far from easy. Rewarding perhaps, not easy.

"Well." Jonah flopped his head down on Trey's chest so he couldn't see him anymore. Which was a shame. He kissed Trey's nipple, sucking it briefly before he lay still.

Trey stroked hair off Jonah's face and a whole-body shiver ran through him. At that Jonah lifted his head, expression now solemn. "Why do you keep doing that?"

"Missed you," Trey said in a low voice.

"Oh." Jonah ducked again, but not before Trey caught his smile. He traced Trey's biceps with a blunt finger. After a lengthy silence, he said, "You'll be gone longer next time, I think."

"Probably," Trey admitted. "I should do more than make phone calls, especially since I can phone from here."

"What would you do if I asked to come with you?"

Something like anguish twisted inside Trey. It was too dangerous. He couldn't afford to put Jonah in danger, not so soon after the near-starvation at the hands of Horton. But he couldn't say no either. Words strangled in his throat as Trey hesitated.

"I see," Jonah said quietly against Trey's skin.

"I can't have them get you again." The words came out hoarse, pleading for understanding.

"We could protect each other. Maybe I don't want them to get *you.*"

Trey knew Jonah had killed Horton, could kill when necessary, and the knowledge was reassuring. Jonah had more resources than Quinn had had, after all. But Jonah was not invincible, not by a long shot.

"I'm glad you don't want them to get me."

"Jesus, Trey, you're impossible." But at least Jonah hadn't stiffened in his arms. In fact his entire body felt malleable under Trey's hands, and Trey thought about what else they could do together.

Jonah noticed and shook his head. "Uh-uh. We're going to finish this conversation first. Don't distract me."

Trey frowned, trying to find the words to talk his lover out of this. "Are you actually ready to go back to a town, to a city?"

Eyeing him, maybe guessing his game, Jonah paused before he admitted, "No. Not yet. I'm talking more about the future."

Relief flowed through Trey. The future, he might be able to make safer for Jonah and himself, might not feel this overwhelming need to prevent Jonah from coming with him. But for now, Jonah could stay safely here, away from Gabriel who would kill him or Kingley who would dissect him.

"I don't want a lifetime of me waiting for you to return."

Jonah rose above him, gazed at Trey, his expression willing Trey to understand. "It's too difficult."

Trey cradled Jonah's face in his hands. They kissed, chaste at first, then deeper, warmer, stronger. Trey broke it off to say, "I don't want that either. We're not going to make that our future."

The next time Trey left, they made frantic love the night before, as if they couldn't get close enough to each other, Trey insisting Jonah fuck him and Jonah only too eager to oblige.

In the days that followed, Jonah missed Trey, but his heart had grown accustomed to absences and in some ways it was easier when he acknowledged to himself that he missed Trey and wanted him to come back.

Then summer was upon them, Trey had returned, and they simply enjoyed each other, forgetting about the future, although Jonah knew about the shadow Trey carried—that Trey was working himself up to tracking down Gabriel and killing him. It was necessary in order to keep the boy Ira safe. Jonah found himself wishing he could take that burden off Trey but didn't know how. During the two times Jonah had mentioned he could help, Trey had become almost panicked about the idea. Not that he showed it. His face turned impassive and his body went still. But Jonah had learned how to scent these things.

So one morning, as summer was ending, Jonah said, "You're going to have to tell me what Gabriel did."

Trey had been relaxing in the sun, and the way his body tensed had Jonah regretting his words, and yet it was something he couldn't help but demand they share. This was eating Trey up inside.

"Gabriel likes to prey on humans. Kill them." Trey stared at the sun, blinding himself perhaps. "He killed my first love."

Jonah blinked. He hadn't known Trey *had* a first love. In his stupid ignorance, he'd thought he was the first, like he was the first one Trey had called a mate. The jealousy that arose in him made him ashamed. Because there was a broken note to Trey's voice.

After Jonah's non-response, Trey added, "I can't really talk about it."

"What was his name?"

Jonah wasn't sure Trey would answer but he reluctantly said, "Quinn."

He had too many questions, from what was Quinn like to why Trey hadn't already killed Gabriel.

Trey guessed something of Jonah's thinking. "At first, I thought Gabriel could be rehabilitated. That he'd fallen in with the wrong crowd, that he was young, that he hadn't realized who Quinn was to me. All sorts of excuses and rationales. Inexcusable, foolhardy. Then later, when I realized what he really was—a vicious killer—he disappeared, avoiding me. He's been hard to corner."

A desire was growing in Jonah to stalk and kill Gabriel. But now he understood that if he told Trey about this urge, Trey would freak, given what had happened to Quinn. Trey could not withstand his brother killing another lover. So instead Jonah asked, "Was he kind to you?"

"Who?"

"Who else? Quinn."

"Yes." The word was said on a sigh. "Patient too, because he didn't know what I was or why I disappeared periodically."

"At least I know."

Trey threw an arm over his face. "At least you know."

Jonah crawled over to rest his head on Trey's other arm and place a hand on Trey's chest. "I'm glad you had someone else. It's always bothered me that you've been alone for so long."

Trey pulled Jonah close. "Not anymore."

"Not anymore."

Jonah shouldn't have been surprised when that winter Trey came home a mess. Gabriel was dead, shot in the head, and if Trey hadn't pulled the trigger, he believed himself responsible for his brother's death, and his miserable life.

All he could do was hold Trey and try to heal him. They talked about the future, and that seemed to help. Neither of them wanted to stay up here in the Canadian Shield forever, as much as it was a kind of cocoon away from the rest of the world.

One evening, Trey floated the idea of Jonah meeting his extended family—eventually. The suggestion made Jonah nervous. He wasn't used to people or being judged by them. On the other hand he liked the idea of meeting people who were important to Trey. Well, he had time to get used to the notion, given Trey's desire to hide Jonah away from humanity indefinitely.

"Once we make things safe," added Trey, ever vigilant about Jonah's safety.

Jonah sighed. "And you'll know when that is?"

"Well." Trey looked down for a moment, grief and anger still within him. "Gabriel's out of the way."

Jonah held his breath, waiting for Trey to withdraw into

himself, into the self-hatred that arose when Gabriel's name was mentioned, but Trey moved on, keeping it matter-of-fact.

"It's Kingley I worry about now."

Kingley, the man Trey had worked most closely with over the years. Jonah was developing a deep dislike of the man. "But you've had no contact with him for more than a year. Can he find you?"

"That's what I don't know. I sometimes feel paranoid using this satellite phone. That he'll track me with it."

"What would he need to be able to track you?"

"He'd need to know this signal is mine. I don't think he can, given where and when I bought it, but...it's hard to be one-hundred-percent sure."

Jonah felt angry, for Trey's sake. Kingley's arm had such a long reach that Trey was always looking over his shoulder. "I wanted to kill Gabriel, you know."

Trey stared at him, shaking his head. "In the oddest way, you are more bloodthirsty than I am."

"I'm only bloodthirsty when it's warranted. But I'll admit it. Stalking the one who needs to be killed gives me, gives the cat inside me, intense satisfaction. You think I am so vulnerable, because you met me when I was more ignorant and naïve than I am now. And I will always be fifteen years younger than you. But I have the patience to kill those who need it. Gabriel needed it."

"I couldn't have stood the idea of you two in the same place and time."

"I know. He killed Quinn. But he didn't kill me." Jonah stroked a hand up Trey's arm. "I'm here."

Trey clasped him in a bear hug. "Quinn taught me how to be in love. So did you."

Jonah mouthed Trey's neck, working his way down to Trey's chest. "I'm jealous of Quinn," he admitted.

"Oh, babe, Quinn would have loved you."

Jonah lifted his head, frowning. "He loved *you*, you idiot. And I'm glad. Just a little jealous. I know it's not reasonable."

Here, Trey laughed. "You are the most reasonable person I've ever met. I don't know how you put up with me." Jonah stopped, staring, tilting his head until Trey said, "What?"

For whatever reason, Trey had not had enough people in his life to love him. Neither had Jonah, perhaps, but his early years had been formed by strong ties with his brother and mother. These had been absent from Trey's world, as far as Jonah could tell. And yet, Jonah remained stingy with certain words, perhaps a kind of leftover punishment for Trey's leaving.

"*What?*" demanded Trey again, and as Jonah was about to say the words he loved to hear from Trey, *I love you*, Trey's sat phone rang.

They gazed at each other. It would only be an emergency, Trey had told him, if that phone rang. Jonah's heart rate sped up and he feared for his lover, for what Trey was about to learn. Slowly, eyes on Jonah, Trey reached for the black rectangle, pushed a button.

"Hello. Trey Walters speaking." He paused. "Who is this?"

Then Jonah watched as Trey's face changed, settled into the expression he got when he was going away. He stared at Jonah as he said, "Hello, Ethan. You've been gone for a very long time."

Ethan. Jonah didn't know that name. But Jonah did know about very long times, and now one was coming. Trey and he were about to be separated.

Chapter Twenty

That summer Jonah gave up on waiting. Too many months had passed. But this time, the anger wasn't there, either because of his own maturity or because he better understood Trey.

When Trey had left the first time, Jonah hadn't really understood or believed in Trey's reluctance to do so. How could he, given the manner of Trey's departure—Jonah sleeping—and the brief time they had known each other.

But this last leave-taking, Jonah had demanded two things—that Trey not slip away and that Trey leave him a contact number Jonah could use if weeks turned to months turned to seasons.

And the season had turned.

So Jonah slipped into the town where he usually bought his supplies and he searched out a payphone. Years ago, his mother had taught him how to use one and while the payphone looked like an updated version of what he'd practiced on, the principles remained the same.

Staring through the plexiglass, he pulled in a long breath, trying to steady his nerves. This situation was too reminiscent of those painful years when he'd believed Trey was dead. But then, unlike now, he hadn't had a number to dial. He stepped up to the payphone and punched in the number.

The third ring cut off as someone picked up, and his hopes rose, like a lifeline was stretching out before him.

"Hello?" came a female voice, clear in his ear.

Not Trey, not even male. Disoriented, Jonah gripped the phone more tightly, trying to think through this unexpected development but unable to form a coherent reply. "Hello?" she repeated, tone a little more demanding this time.

"Hello," he echoed, figuring he couldn't go wrong with the one word, wondering if he had to be careful not to give something away to this woman who'd answered Trey's number. At the same time a part of Jonah was thinking, *If Trey gave me just any shit number, I am going to kill him.*

"Can I help you?" she said into the silence.

Jonah made himself loosen his grip on the phone before he broke it, and cleared his throat. "Yes, please. Uh..." *Christ.* "Who's speaking, please?"

"You called here, remember?" The tone wasn't annoyed so much as chiding, a little confused. "Who are you?"

He paused, debating the pros and cons of offering his name to her. In the end, he refused to hang up, refused to let go of his only connection to Trey. "I'm Jonah."

"*Jonah.*" She sounded suddenly intent, as if his name meant something to her. "I've been hoping you would call."

"You have?" he asked, hoping this meant she had good news for him. "I mean, who is this?" *Do you know Trey?* But Jonah didn't want to give Trey's name away, not when Trey had been so worried about Kingley's ability to find him.

"I'm Veronica, Trey's niece."

Okay. Veronica. Trey spoke fondly of her, and of all his kin, it sounded like Trey had the best rapport with her. But Jonah wasn't entirely sure why Trey had given him *her* number instead of his. It was a sleight of hand, and he didn't like it. "Do you know where Trey is?"

She sighed. "No. And that's the problem."

"He's mentioned you."

"Just mentioned?" she said dryly.

"Well..." Trey didn't tend to discuss people.

"Never mind, Trey's not a big talker, I know." She switched topics. "Look, the thing is, we were kind of hoping he'd gone back to wherever you are. He's been a bit secretive about your location. You know how he is."

Jonah sometimes wondered if he knew how Trey was at all, but that was not a point to be debated here and now. "Do you have any way to contact him? His sat phone number, for example."

She hesitated. "He doesn't want us to use that, Jonah."

"Explain to me why."

"It's been compromised. Whoever he used to work for has the ability to use it to trace it back to us."

"Please give it to me."

"He won't be answering it anymore," she argued. "It'll be rerouted to someone else, probably someone dangerous."

Jonah leaned his forehead against the plexiglass. "I don't care who answers it, if they lead me to Trey."

She didn't say anything.

"Veronica?"

Her voice went smaller. "He'll never forgive me if they harm you."

Jonah strived to say the most persuasive thing possible, but all that came out was the truth. "He's tired."

"Pardon?"

"Trey is tired. Of working, of killing. He didn't want to go back. He might need help getting out. *I* can help him."

"Jonah, no offense, but you're only human. You don't understand what you're up against."

Here he smiled to himself. "Trey lied about that. I'm not only human."

A long pause then, as though she was processing that information, weighing it. "I may never know if you're lying or not."

"*I* don't lie. Trey is the one who doesn't know how to live without secrets and deception."

She let out a long breath and it sounded like surrender. "Are you sure?"

"Yes, I am sure. I can help him. Give me the number, Veronica. Don't you think he deserves some help? Don't you think he takes too much on his own shoulders?"

He heard her swear to herself. Then she got defensive. "We considered one of us using the number, we gave ourselves a deadline of this October, because Trey's been gone six months before easily. But we're all raising families, we're all interconnected. To put the children at risk..."

"I absolutely understand," he assured her. "I have no children. I only have Trey. I want him back, and I can do this."

"Are you a wolf then?"

He considered saying lynx, then remembered he was the only one known to exist and she might not believe him. So he said, "Cat."

"That makes sense. Trey's more cat than wolf, I sometimes think."

She was obviously hungry to know more about Trey, and while Jonah wasn't unsympathetic, finding Trey was the priority. "Veronica..."

He thought he'd have to ask again, but then she was telling him the number and he was memorizing it.

If it were up to him, Trey would have left months ago. But first there'd been a feral wolf to be found and brought back to humanity, and then a dysfunctional pack to run until a member of said pack emerged as the alpha. So instead of returning to Jonah, Trey had been trying to save lives. The blood of too many feral or psychopathic werewolves were already on his hands. He had done what he could to avoid more.

So as he washed the blood off his arms and chest, the irony of what he'd finished here didn't escape him. Sure he'd just killed a murderer. Kingley wasn't stupid. He only assigned wetwork Trey could stomach. But lately Trey found even that was difficult for him to carry out.

Being with Jonah had made him soft. But he didn't want to think about Jonah, especially not now.

Instead he focused on what he'd accomplished in the past months. The feral wolf was back in civilization, living in a house with his partner, and the pack had a new leader who, while young, was strong and sane.

Trey should have been free to leave, having accomplished what he needed to accomplish for his kin. Instead of going home, however, Trey had gotten himself tangled in Kingley's web. This time he didn't know quite how to extricate himself without causing harm.

The wolf pack had changed the balance of power. Before, Kingley had never had anything to hold over Trey, who'd been careful not to cultivate ties. But Trey had grown to feel responsible for the pack and its members, and Kingley had zeroed in on those feelings. He'd been aware of the pack's existence, of course. Within the U.S., there were three known to

214

the government. But now Kingley could hold the lives and well-being of these members over Trey's head.

The government was still extremely uneasy about the existence of werewolves and despite rumors that had spread into the general population, werewolves were generally held to be as real as UFOs at this point.

Kingley threatened to change that and Trey did not want a mob descending upon the pack, turning a confrontation into a bloodbath. He didn't know if Kingley would truly do such a thing, or if Kingley just liked having Trey under his power. He'd done this work to essentially appease Kingley, but he couldn't keep it up. Jonah would never forgive him if he didn't return, and soon. And Jonah didn't deserve to be left hanging like this—again. Trey dried his hands and put in a call.

"Done," he said, no preamble. He expected another assignment to be given, and maybe that would suffice and they could declare things even.

"There's been a development," said Kingley, in that tone of voice that indicated he was excited. How this would affect Trey, he didn't yet know, but it didn't bode well. "Come back in."

Before this phone call, Trey would have been happy to have his killing spree cut short, but now all he felt was suspicion at this turn of events.

"Where are we meeting?" Trey demanded.

"The usual."

His wolf balked. Trey didn't want to return to the compound. One of these days, he would never be allowed to leave. "No."

"You'll do as I say."

That was new. Kingley avoided ultimatums. "A safe house, Shaun."

"No."

Monosyllabic negatives on either side wasn't good. His wolf rose, fighting Kingley's attempt to back him into a corner. His instincts screamed no. If he lost all leverage with Kingley, he'd be in no position to protect the pack or anyone else. He'd simply be helpless and Kingley could harm anyone he pleased.

Like hell that was going to happen.

"Yes," answered Trey. "I'll be at the Birchwood Street house in two days."

Trey hung up and turned off the phone. As he slipped it into his pocket, he wondered if he'd have to kill Kingley. He didn't want to, had worked too long with the man, even if a lot of it had been bad.

But he no longer trusted Kingley. Maybe he never had. Still Trey knew when Kingley was making a power move, and this was one.

"I have someone who wants to see you. Jonah Carvin is his name." Kingley turned to Jonah as he spoke into the newly dead line. Kingley thought Jonah was human, thought it was a werewolf who had torn Horton's throat, and Kingley didn't know that Jonah could hear that Trey was no longer there.

Kingley's eyebrows lifted as he regarded Jonah. "Trey hung up. He doesn't want to see you."

It was easy to sound uncertain. Jonah would never be a great actor, but he could always sound unsure of himself. "I don't think that's true."

"It's a reasonable conclusion. Yet you told me you were important to Trey."

Jonah looked away so his contempt wouldn't shine through. He had said no such thing, had said little about Trey.

"Well. Trey won't come here." There was a certain disgruntlement in Kingley's smile. "So we will go to Trey."

Jonah continued to stare at the floor, because now he feared triumph would show in his eyes. The guard, one of two men who had stayed with him 24/7 ever since Jonah had dialed in Trey's sat phone number, gestured, and Jonah preceded him out the door. Kingley didn't bother with niceties such as saying hello or goodbye, or even dismissed.

The guard was a problem though. Jonah was only stalking one man, and he didn't want another harmed during his campaign.

It had been simple to get in touch with Kingley. As soon as Jonah had called the number Veronica had given him, asking for Trey, he'd been transferred to Kingley, who in turn was very interested in anyone who had access to Trey's private phone number. Jonah had obligingly given out his location—he'd made a point of traveling days away from the town near home. Within hours, someone had met him, ostensibly in a friendly way, but as soon as he was in the interior of that car, he recognized he was a prisoner.

He'd been prepared for that. His biggest fear had been that someone would realize he was a lynx, somehow put two and two together since Horton's death. But whoever that first guard with Horton had been—Trey'd said his name was Leonard—he hadn't passed on enough information to Kingley to allow him to guess Jonah was Horton's former prisoner. Probably because Horton had wanted Jonah to be his secret.

Secrets, secrets, and more secrets. That seemed to be what Trey's work was about. No wonder Trey was not the most forthcoming guy in the world. Years of playing these games, it would affect you, it had affected Trey.

Jonah wondered if Trey had ever been where he was staying, in this large mansion in a gated area. Not great for shapeshifters, no real place to run, no way to easily slip in and out of the community.

Didn't matter now as he was bundled into yet another bulletproof car—his guard was chattier than Leonard had ever been—and driven towards Trey, towards this Birchwood address.

They stopped for food on the way, the guard with them. Till now, Jonah hadn't actually spent much time with Kingley, but during the ten-hour drive, Jonah began to realize that Kingley was not exactly Horton. If this was imprisonment, it was on a completely different level than what had happened with Horton. Clearly Kingley was manipulative, but the lynx within was losing its enthusiasm for the stalking and killing. Because Kingley was not trying to bring death to anyone.

Aaron had killed Jonah's mother and Horton had been slowly killing Jonah himself, had been out for Trey's blood. But Kingley, while he'd been an asshole on the phone to Trey, might not be evil.

Before he acted, Jonah needed to understand what power Kingley held over Trey and why. And destroy it, one way or the other.

Chapter Twenty-One

Trey had chosen the Birchwood Street safe house because he knew he could reach it before Kingley. And he didn't want any surprises. He checked out the place for himself first, to ensure it was empty, grabbing some clothing and a gun while he was at it. Then he hunkered down outside to wait and see who arrived.

Trey had always been very careful with himself and his killings, always making sure he had good reason before he took another's life. He didn't *want* to kill his old boss. Not that he trusted or liked Kingley, but he'd worked with the man over the years and through that relationship had been allowed to accomplish a lot for his fellow shapeshifters.

Kingley was making vague threats about the pack, but till now Trey had believed the threat was not real so much as heavy-handed manipulation, made to ensure that Trey "paid back" Kingley's latest favor—which had involved setting free a shapeshifting cougar. So Trey had obliged for a time, but it simply couldn't go on.

Either Kingley had to pull back or Trey had to move forward and act. As he examined the gun again, a sense of dread enveloped him. He was too old for this, too old for games. This had to end, one way or the other.

He waited through the night, allowing himself the lightest

of sleep, always keeping one ear open. The car pulled into the driveway early the next morning, bringing Trey to full alert. Kingley exited the car first but behind him, from the passenger seat, a terribly familiar body emerged from the car and Trey's heart seized. *Jonah.*

He couldn't think. He heard his throat growling, low, barely audible. Jonah was *not* supposed to be here. Trey felt as if somehow Kingley had let a cougar go only to go behind his back and bag a lynx, his lynx. This had *never* been part of the deal.

It could not be allowed. His growl grew stronger.

Jonah glanced his way though Trey didn't think he'd been loud enough for even a lynx's hearing.

"What are you looking at?" Kingley asked, and Jonah turned his gaze away from the small clump of woods beside the house.

There was one guard, who was instructed to stay outside and keep an eye on the surroundings while Jonah and Kingley went into the house. Once his heart stopped thundering, Trey managed to observe that Jonah didn't appear to feel threatened and Kingley wasn't acting threatening. This was nothing resembling the Horton bunker and Jonah's near-starvation, but how had these two gotten together and what the fuck was happening?

Trey waited fifteen long minutes until the guard did a desultory round of the house. Then he slipped into the now-unlocked house. He crept silently forward, listening for conversation, for action, for signs of Jonah's well-being. At the doorway to the living room, Trey stopped to see Kingley rifling through the desk while Jonah sat calmly on the couch.

Their gazes met, those green eyes making Trey weak and strong, hot and cold—how had Jonah managed to arrive here? Trey's wolf pushed towards the surface, wanting to take over, wanting to protect his mate.

But Jonah was not surprised to see Trey. He gave the briefest shake of his head like Trey had done something wrong. And then, to Trey's utter surprise, he said, "It's time."

Kingley looked at Jonah who lifted his chin to indicate Trey. Kingley jerked, his entire body stiffening with surprise.

"Jesus, I didn't hear you." He reached for something on the desk.

"Don't call the guard," Jonah said quietly and Kingley frowned, as if Jonah was acting out of character even while Jonah moved with lynx speed to intercept Kingley's hand, and took the phone for himself. "It will only be the three of us. That's best."

Trey was watching Jonah now, remembering old conversations where Jonah had spoken of killing Kingley. There was something unsettlingly intense in Jonah's expression.

Kingley opened his mouth to yell and Trey said harshly, "Shut it or he might kill you," as Jonah rose again and reached for Kingley, bringing his large hand to wrap around Kingley's throat.

"Jonah," Trey warned.

"Only the three of us," Jonah repeated, his voice showing little emotion.

Kingley's face burnt red with anger and he said thickly, given Jonah's hand, "Who the fuck are you?"

"I'm a friend of Trey's."

"*Friend*," Kingley sneered.

"Unlike, say, you. You need to leave Trey alone from here on in."

"Jonah," Trey repeated.

He laid his strangely reassuring gaze on Trey. "I'm not out of control." Then he turned back to Kingley. "Will you stay quiet, or should I stay here?"

Kingley slung his eyes towards Trey. "Control your pet dog."

"He's no dog," said Trey, "but he's dangerous. Tell him you'll stay quiet."

"I won't be yelling," Kingley told Jonah after a pause, his expression furious.

Eyeing Kingley carefully, Jonah released him and stepped back.

Kingley rubbed his throat. "What is going on, Trey?"

"I was going to ask the same thing," replied Trey. "You wanted me to come to the compound. Why?" Kingley didn't answer, just tilted his head at Jonah. "You were going to keep Jonah prisoner there?"

"I thought I was bringing you an old friend," protested Kingley as he edged closer to the desk. He must have left his gun in a drawer there.

"Stop," Trey said flatly, and his old boss knew him well enough to stop.

"Should I kill him?" Jonah asked mildly. Kingley's flinch was barely discernible but Trey observed it. "What hold does he have on you? Because I need to break it."

It was the completely wrong timing, but something within Trey trembled to know that Jonah did not blame Trey for the long absence, was not furious at being left behind again. Jonah believed that Trey had been forced to stay away from him. Trey rubbed his face, unable to speak for the moment.

"None whatsoever," said Kingley.

"You're a terrible liar." Jonah pulled in a long breath. "I can smell the lie on you. But it doesn't matter. Trey and I are leaving now. If you ever contact him again, I will find you and kill you."

222

Kingley snorted dismissively.

"I killed Horton."

At that, Kingley froze while Trey winced. "I wish you hadn't said that, Jonah."

Jonah kept his gaze on Kingley, deadly serious and perhaps that was finally sinking in. "He needs to know I mean it."

"He's threatened the well-being of a pack of wolves I've tried to rehabilitate," Trey said quickly.

"Bullshit," declared Kingley, trying to regain control of the conversation. "I did you a fucking huge favor, Walters, and for that I get this grief."

Trey stared at Kingley. "You were going to use Jonah against me. I don't think I can forgive that."

Kingley paled. He'd seen Trey in action before, recognized that tone of voice.

"But here's the thing. I don't want to kill you. I've killed too much and we, well, we've worked together. But you crossed a line here. I think you need to understand that."

Jonah stepped forward. "I'll kill him, not you." The words were like a gift that everyone in the room understood and this time Kingley's flinch was obvious. Jonah's mouth curved sardonically. "If you ever contact Trey again, or harm these wolves he's talking about, I will find you. And if, somehow, I can't get near you, another shifter will. We're a stealthy bunch. You will never be safe if I decide you need to be eliminated."

Kingley blinked once, and Trey waited for a counterargument, something that would bind Trey and Kingley together.

There was only silence. And with something like amazement, Trey realized it was time to go.

"Watch him," Trey told Jonah. "I think there's a gun in the desk and he was reaching for it."

Jonah nodded. "I'm watching."

Trey retrieved rope and a gag, and they tied up a now-silent Kingley. It was an odd way to say goodbye after twenty years, but Trey didn't want any more conversation. Kingley had always managed to run circles around him when it came to words.

He looked into Kingley's eyes and they were blazing.

Trey put his face right in Kingley's, this one last time. "Stay away from me and mine, Shaun. This is your final warning."

Kingley blinked once before Jonah's hand was on Trey's arm, leading him out the back door.

Evading the guard as they exited the house took no effort. In the small copse of the woods they embraced wordlessly but then something within Trey let loose and he pulled away to shake the lynx roughly. "You *fuckhead*, Jonah. He could have killed you."

All Jonah did was shush him with pets and kisses as he said, "We don't have a lot of time."

"I didn't want you to ever get near this shit again." Somehow Trey couldn't stop himself from delivering this furious lecture, though he knew they had to shift and get out of here. This naivety of Jonah's scared the shit out of him. He couldn't afford to have anything more to do with his old life if it was going to bring Jonah's lynx nature to the fore, prowling in here to rescue Trey. Next time, people might bring Jonah down—and eviscerate him. The idea was simply unbearable.

Jonah grabbed hold of Trey's face, cradling him in his hands, reminding him that his lover was warm and alive and smiling, right in front of him. "Listen to me, Trey. It's over, okay? You can scold me later."

"I've lost it. *I can't do this anymore.*"

"I know." Jonah smoothed hair off Trey's forehead. "So you're not doing this anymore. Now, shift."

Jonah lay on top of him, almost squeezing the air out of his chest, yet the pressure of his body on Trey's gave him such pleasure. While Trey had trouble admitting it to himself, this was perhaps what he loved most, lying beneath Jonah's hard body.

Jonah pressed a palm against Trey's rough stubble, and Trey responded. He didn't purr like Jonah sometimes did, but Jonah sensed his reaction and smiled.

"Who said you're a whore for punishment again?"

Trey turned into Jonah's palm, in part to avoid his gaze, then murmured, "You know who."

"What did Quinn mean by that?"

"He thought I was too hard on myself and my body. But he didn't know I was a werewolf."

"So were you punishing yourself by continuing to work for Kingley?"

The post-sex glow began to fade and Trey became disgruntled. "Don't psychoanalyze me for God's sake."

"Well, that's my theory. That or you were happy to get away from me."

Trey gripped Jonah's arms and moved quickly to flip them over, so he was on top now. But his anger simply disappeared as Jonah grinned up at him. "But *I* think you missed me."

To Trey's horror, his eyes welled up.

"Jesus, Trey," and Jonah pulled him down into a hug. "I think you're a big softy who got the shit beat out of him too young and for too long. But now you're with me and we're going to live a very sedate life while I study math and you..."

Trey pushed back and pounded the cot beside them. "You could have been *killed*."

Jonah wasn't cowed by the outburst. "Yes, I think you've mentioned that once or twice."

"You don't understand how close you came. If Kingley had realized *at all* that you weren't human..."

"But he didn't, did he?"

Trey shook his head and gave up trying to explain.

"I think, Trey, that your life may have been in danger a time or two over the years."

Jonah, as usual, was missing the point. "Never because of you. I brought you to this."

"Because you were helping people you care about." Jonah's voice went lower. "I'm allowed to do that too."

"Not anymore."

Jonah laughed.

"It's not fucking funny."

"It's not funny," Jonah agreed. "But remember, we're heading for the quiet life now. I'm studying math and you... What are you going to do?"

"I don't have to do anything." Trey sank back down so he was talking to Jonah's shoulder which was somehow easier than looking into Jonah's too-keen gaze. "I've saved a lot of money over the years. We'll use some of that to buy a house for winter, so you can study and I can rest. Honestly, I'm so tired, I just want a break." He let out a huge sigh, still exhausted after their week-long trek back home.

"Okay, house-buying it is." Jonah wrapped arms around Trey, holding him close. "But sleep first."

Trey turned his face into Jonah's neck and listened to the pulse of his lover's heart beat deep and strong. It was music to his senses, and like music, it lulled him to sleep.

A Note From the Author

Trey has been in every single one of my books set in this world, and it was quite a challenge writing *Lynx* because I needed to track a rather complicated timeline! He stepped on to the page during Kir and Josh's story—*Monster, Zombie*, and *Minder* which comprise the print book *Beautiful Monster*. And it was over the course of these books that Trey had to be away from Jonah for so long as he infiltrated the Agency.

I always wondered about Trey during those times he would make an appearance in others' lives, and I wrote *Lynx* to find out what was going on in his life. Events that shape the later part of *Lynx*, including the rescue of Ira and the killing of Gabriel, take place in *Marked*, Liam and Alec's story. And, near the end of *Lynx* when Trey gets a phone call from Ethan and goes on to save a feral wolf (Bram)—that occurs in *Feral*. Needless to say much that occurred in previous books affected Trey and Jonah's relationship.

As well, I've written books under my Jorrie Spencer name, and Trey appears in them too. That's where you'll see his niece Veronica's story, in *The Strength of the Wolf*.

Lynx doesn't necessarily mean Trey won't be in future stories that I write, but he will be with Jonah and working at a further remove. He is (mostly) retired and no longer putting his life in danger.

About the Author

To learn more about Joely Skye, please visit www.joelyskye.com. Send an email to Joely at Joely.Skye@gmail.com or join her Yahoo group groups.yahoo.com/group/joelyskye.

Seduction is his only chance for freedom...
and love is a death sentence.

Feral
© *2009 Joely Skye*

Even among shifters, Ethan is a rare breed. So rare, he's spent the last eight years in hiding from the werewolves who once captured and tortured him. Now a tranq dart has cut short his feral existence. Waking in human form in a locked room is more than a living nightmare...it's reliving his worst one.

Yet in the troubled eyes of one of his captors, he senses a weak link. One he can use to escape—by seducing his jailer.

Bram's life as pack omega isn't easy. As long as he obeys his alpha he is protected. However, there are some things he just can't bring himself to do. Keeping a precious cougar shifter prisoner is one of them, especially one who has somehow managed to capture his heart.

Setting Ethan free could be a death sentence for both of them, for Bram's pack doesn't take betrayal lightly. And the alpha is set on revenge.

Warning: Explicit m/m sex and violence.

Available now in ebook and print from Samhain Publishing.

LaVergne, TN USA
14 January 2011
212444LV00008B/1/P